☆THE☆ STAR-SPANGLED SECRET

K. M. KIMBALL

ALADDIN PAPERBACKS
New York London Toronto Sydney Singapore

First Aladdin Paperbacks edition October 2001

Aladdin Paperbacks
An imprint of Simon & Schuster
Children's Publishing Division
1230 Avenue of the Americas
New York, NY 10020

Designed by Lisa Vega
The text of this book was set in Adobe Caslon Regular.
Printed and bound in the United States
10 9 8 7 6 5 4 3 2 1
Library of Congress Cataloging-in-Publication Data:
Kimball, K. M.
The star-spangled secret / by K. M. Kimball
p. cm.
Summary: In 1814, as the War of 1812 threatens her Maryland home, thirteen-year-old Caroline sets out to discover the truth about the disappearance of her older brother.
ISBN: 0-689-84550-2
1. Maryland—History—War of 1812—Juvenile fiction.
[1. Brothers and sisters—Fiction. 2. Maryland—History—War of 1812—Fiction. 3. United States—History—War of 1812—Fiction. 4. Mystery and detective stories.] I. Title
PZ7.J434 Car 2001
[Fic]—dc21 2001033393

☆ ACKNOWLEDGMENTS ☆

This is a book I've wanted to write for a long time. It is the kind of story I loved to read when I was young—full of danger, mystery, and brave (or sometimes strange) characters. My love of history and fascination with America's growth from a handful of colonies dictated that the tale should take place sometime after the Revolution. And what better time than during the War of 1812, when we struggled to save this brand-new country . . . and nearly lost her.

I must thank all of those who helped make this story real and fun, while guarding historical accuracy. To Ellen Krieger, my editor, who catches my mistakes and loves history as much as I do, my deep gratitude. To my critical readers, who are always right—Alice Leonhardt, Chassie West, Linda Hayes, and Helen Chappell—I couldn't have done it without you! To the wonderful staff at Fort McHenry in Baltimore, who know about everything from flags to cannons—I am indebted to you for your answers to my questions. Any errors made in this novel are my own . . . I should have listened harder.

☆CONTENTS☆

☆ PHILADELPHIA AND ☆ BAD NEWS

THE LETTER DANGLED FROM MY TREMBLING FINGER-tips as tears rushed down my cheeks. I couldn't swallow, couldn't breathe through my sobbing. For many grim minutes, life ceased to exist for me. Charlie, my only brother, had drowned.

My friend Amelia found me sitting alone in the gloomy parlor of Mrs. Brown's boardinghouse. Most of us from other cities attending Madame Grelaud's School for Girls in Philadelphia lived here during the eleven months of our school year. "Caroline," she whispered in her soft French accent, so that my name sounded like Car-o-leen, "*ma chérie,* I looked for you everyplace."

I shrugged, unable to answer because my throat burned as if I'd swallowed scalding tea. A hollow, hopeless ache chewed from inside my stomach as teardrops slipped from my chin and the tip of my nose. They plopped on the single page of Mama's pale gray vellum. When I tried to wipe the moisture away, the deep black curls of several letters blurred, pulling my eyes back to the horrible words: *Baltimore Harbor . . . stormy night . . . drowned . . . so very sorry . . . immense grief.*

"Mrs. Brown told me a messenger brought you a letter. She said you were upset, so it must be dreadful news."

I nodded and let her take me into her arms for comfort.

After I had wept myself dry, Amelia helped me sit up. She smoothed out the wrinkles I'd crushed into her pretty silk skirt, embroidered with rosebuds of shining threads in pink and crimson. "It is your mother, *chérie*?" Her eyes were soft and worried. "She is ill with the yellow fever again?"

"No," I said sadly, pressing my lips closed, for I didn't wish to talk of those horrid days, either. "It's not the fever."

The yellow fever had struck during an early, unusually warm spring of 1814 and was the reason Mama had moved us from Philadelphia to Maryland. She herself had nearly perished from it, and I had been too ill to leave my bed for many weeks. But my baby sister, Rebecca, had died. So had poor Papa. "With only Charlie and you left," Mama told me through her misery, "I dare not risk another summer in this cursed city."

We left our beautiful house on Congress Street and moved what belongings we could pile into a coach and two market wagons to Grandpapa Streck's plantation in Maryland. It was called Elk Ridge, and rested on a pretty hill covered in honeysuckle vines and graceful locust trees, midway between Baltimore and Washington City.

But I soon missed my friends so much, I begged to be allowed to return to school. Only when Madame Grelaud herself promised she would remove her students from the city at the slightest threat of another fever outbreak had Mama allowed me to return to Philadelphia.

"No," I repeated hollowly, "it's not Mama. It's Charlie, my brother." I laid the letter in her lap. He had been just fourteen years of age, only one year older than I was. He had been my best friend in all the world. Better even than Amelia.

Amelia read silently for a moment, her lips moving, her eyes widening with horror. "Oh, Caroline. Oh," was all she said when she finished.

"Yes." I sighed, then shook my head and took the letter back from her to read it again. Something about it bothered me. "I don't understand," I murmured at last.

"Understand what?" she asked. "*Vôtre mère,* her letter . . . it says he slipped and fell overboard during the night. Dear Charlie. How terribly sad it is. If I must die—which, of course, I shall someday—I would not choose to drown. All that water rushing—"

"Something's wrong," I interrupted, twisting around to face her. My heart took desperate leaps inside my chest, although I couldn't put words to my feelings.

She fluttered her pale eyelashes in astonishment. "Wrong?"

"Yes." I read the sickening words again quickly, then shoved the page back at her. "Read it aloud to me," I implored her.

Amelia held the creamy sheet delicately between her thin white fingers. She read in a formal, unaccented tone—the one she used in class when she didn't want to sound French, because some of the girls were mean and teased her, calling her Little Miss Bonaparte.

"'I regret to inform you, dearest daughter, that your brother, Charles Chester Dorsey, has perished by drowning. His ship, the *Liberty,* was moored in Baltimore Harbor on the fifteenth of July, this year of our Lord, 1814, due to the British blockade.'"

We had been at war with England for two years now. Hoping to stop our naval and merchant ships from leaving port to bring supplies to our citizens or ammunition to our gunships, the British navy had seized the narrow entrance from the Chesapeake Bay to Baltimore Harbor. The British were also at war with France and often seized or sank American merchant ships if they seemed headed for that country.

Amelia continued. "'It was sometime during that stormy night that Charles fell from the deck into the unforgiving waters. The captain, Mr. Zachariah Moses, came to me with the sad news. Although he personally was not on deck at the time of the accident, he assures me that valiant efforts were made to save Charles. The boy slipped beneath the water and was never to be seen again. You will recall that Captain Moses came highly recommended to us, and he expresses his deepest remorse—'"

"*There,* you see?" I interrupted.

Amelia folded the letter in her lap and stared blankly at me. "See what?"

"It makes no sense, what Mama has been told."

"I think her letter makes perfect sense," Amelia said softly. "You just don't want to believe Charlie is dead."

"If he's dead, it isn't because he *fell* overboard," I stated emphatically, pushing up from the green brocade sofa. "Or that he drowned." I couldn't help thinking that the captain must have been misinformed by his crew as to the details of that dreadful night, for he obviously didn't know my brother as well as I knew him.

The large, high-ceilinged room was lit only by two brass oil lamps on crouching mahogany tables of Chippendale style. Shadows grew long and solemn from their clawed feet, draping themselves across the pianoforte where Amelia's nimble fingers entertained students and guests nearly every night. I had been asked to play no more, for I missed too many keys and made ugly music.

"Charlie could walk a tree branch as narrow as my wrist without losing his balance, and he was a wonderful swimmer," I reasoned. "Even if it were possible for him to fall off a ship's deck, it would have been nothing to him. He would have laughed at his own clumsiness, pulled himself out of the water, and shaken himself dry like a puppy."

"*Oui, mais vôtre mère,* in her letter—"

I waved off her arguments. "I won't believe he could have fallen . . . but he might have been pushed or kidnapped."

Amelia blinked in astonishment. "Kidnapped?"

"Yes!" I paced the carpet excitedly, feeling a surge of hope flowing like a spoonful of warm molasses stirred through curdled milk to make it drinkable. "He might yet be alive, smuggled aboard a British frigate and forced to labor there."

"You mean, impressed? I have read of such things, of course." But she looked doubtful.

"It's possible," I insisted. "Baltimore Harbor is blockaded by the British, is it not? American ships can neither enter nor escape as long as our enemy's fleet controls the Chesapeake Bay. Like all the other American ships in the harbor, the *Liberty* can't get past the blockade to reach the sea. But a British raiding party might have snuck aboard Charlie's ship at night, captured him, and—"

Amelia seized my wrist when my pacing brought me within her reach. She pulled me to a stop, her pale blue eyes fixing solemnly on my face. "No, Caroline. You are making up these fantasies. What good would one cabin boy do them? If the British took Charlie, they'd have made away with more sailors than just him. And the rest of the crew—would they not have heard or seen what was happening, stopped them if they could, or reported the crime? Do you suppose Charlie would have gone quietly, without *une bataille*, a fight? And you are forgetting that the captain's letter speaks of efforts to save Charlie."

I groaned with frustration and shook off her hand. "I suppose you're right about the British taking him from the ship. But I still don't believe he drowned due to his own missed footing. After all, the captain wasn't there to witness his actual disappearance. And sailors have been known to invent tales, particularly to cover up their own misdeeds. What if Charlie argued with someone and he pushed my brother overboard? Charlie might have swum to shore, then been captured by British raiders and taken to that awful old Dartmoor Prison in England, falsely accused of being a deserter from the Royal Navy! Papa used to tell us of hundreds of innocent American sailors seized by the British navy, never to be seen by their families again."

Amelia sighed. "I know, Caroline. But it seems so unlikely, under the circumstances."

But I was unwilling to give up. "My brother could *not* have drowned," I insisted. "And if he didn't drown, he must be somewhere other than on the *Liberty.* He would contact us if he could; he must be in trouble. He must be somewhere needing our help. Surely you can understand that much!"

My head throbbed, and I pressed my fists against my closed eyes, forcing back another gush of tears.

Amelia rose and stood beside me. "You can do nothing about it," she whispered, her accent thick again, soothing. *"Rien du tout. C'est fini."*

"It *isn't* over!" I drew a deep breath and met Amelia's eyes, feeling stronger and more determined than I had a right to be. "I will find out what happened to my brother."

☆ GOING HOME ☆

MAMA'S LETTER HAD SAID I WOULD HAVE TO WAIT ten days for a carriage from Elk Ridge. But I ached to begin questioning anyone who might have knowledge of Charlie's reported drowning. I couldn't very well do that from more than one hundred miles away in Philadelphia.

I wrote asking that I be allowed to book passage on a public coach. One left nearly every day for Baltimore, and such things were easily arranged. Mrs. Brown even said she'd help me. Return post brought Mama's answer: *Patience, my child,* she wrote, *patience. I do not want you traveling alone by public transport during these dangerous times, and I cannot immediately spare a driver. With the wheat and tobacco nearing harvest, I shall require every hand for the fields. Without crops to sell, there will be no money to run this household.*

"If Grandpapa Streck weren't away," I complained bitterly to Amelia, "he would come for me himself."

"He is still in Europe?" she asked.

"He left for Belgium this spring, entrusting his property and investments to Mama's care. With Napoléon imprisoned on Elba, he felt it a good time to try to reclaim land taken from our family during the war in Europe."

In this most recent letter, Mama also wrote of her fears that we might be forced to leave Elk Ridge if frightening rumors proved true. Baltimore and Washington City, our capital, hadn't been troubled by foreign troops since the War of the Revolution, before I was born. But as soon as President Madison officially declared the United States at war with England, in the summer of 1812, everyone panicked.

People began talking of the king's soldiers marching through our streets just as brazenly as they had raided farms to the far north and west of us.

Lately, I had read in Papa's favorite newspaper, the *National Intelligencer,* of the most dangerous threat yet to America. Thousands of freshly trained British soldiers were reported by American spies to be sailing across the Atlantic Ocean from England. They would be added to many hundreds of enemy troops already in Canada or waiting in ships just off our shores.

While I watched for the carriage to arrive, I tried to keep my mind on my schoolwork. But, like everyone else in our young country, I couldn't stop fearing the worst. Would the hated Redcoats dare drive us from our homes? Or, worse still, murder us in our beds? I lay awake nights, glad for the thick brick walls and heavy slate roof of Mrs. Brown's house. I shivered at terrifying visions of blasting muskets and long, sharp bayonets. And day after grim day, I also dwelt miserably on July 15, the night Charlie was said to have drowned.

I tried to envision my brother standing on the

ship's deck. What sort of night had it been? Dreary and sinisterly dark, then the sky ablaze with sudden, terrifying lightning as a storm blew in across the harbor? Bright, clear, and cool, with a fat, silvery moon and no wind at all? Or had the air been hot and still . . . sticky, clinging, and secretive, before blowing in so unexpectedly that Charlie had been swept off his feet? I wished with all my heart that I had been there with Charlie to see what had transpired that fateful night. To learn the truth.

One thing I did know for certain: If Charlie had died that night or any other, I would have sensed that I had lost him. I would have *felt* something. Somehow I would have understood, just as I'd understood about Papa and Rebecca.

Days before my father breathed his last breath, I realized he was leaving us. No matter how often he patted my hand and whispered to me faintly from his bed that he would be well again, that we would ride together . . . I knew he would never again sit a horse.

And when little Becky also fell to the fever, I

sensed death hovering evilly over us again. Before her tiny cornflower-blue eyes dulled and became swallowed up in her fever-swollen face, before the doctor came to bleed her with his noxious leeches to remove the poisons from her body, I understood she was not to be spared. I held her in my arms, singing softly to her, all the last night she spent on this earth. So I was sure I would have sensed if Charlie was lost to me.

Dear Charlie. He was destined to be a good seaman because he loved the water more than the land. He knew the name of every ship that sailed, even before he was apprenticed to the *Liberty*. "That one's a sloop!" he would cry out when he was just eight years old. "And there's a grand old frigate—a forty-four gunner, I'd guess!"

Once, when he was eleven and the whole family traveled to Baltimore, he identified every ship he saw in the harbor. First, a massive man-o'-war; then a speedy cutter; a square-rigged brig; a sleek, shore-hugging schooner; and scores more. All Charlie required was a quick glimpse of angled masts, unfurled sails, and the telltale curve of a hull. But it was just a game for him until a year ago.

Just before Papa fell ill, Charlie had started talking of signing on as a cabin boy with a privateer ship, to fight for our country. Privateers weren't in the real American navy. They were privately owned ships given special permission by our Congress to attack British ships during wartime. Charlie's fascination with these legalized pirates eventually resulted in his being signed on to one of them, although it would be many months later, under unexpected circumstances.

Now, with each day that passed as I waited to return to Elk Ridge, my sense that Charlie still lived grew stronger. I became more and more certain a terrible mistake had been made, although I had no proof of it. What had happened to my brother if indeed he had fallen from the deck of the *Liberty*? Why had there been no sign, no word of him at all? Charlie would know that Mama and I were worrying; he'd find a way to reassure us that he was alive . . . if he could.

"Maybe he needs our help to bargain for his freedom from the wicked British," I suggested to Amelia.

"They might be holding him at their base on Tangier Island at the south end of the bay! Or he might be injured, unable to make his way back to us!"

She only shook her head sadly.

At last, a stable boy named Foley arrived with Grandpapa's best barouche to carry me back to Maryland. "We will drive through the night to make as much speed as possible," I told him as I settled myself impatiently on the tufted velvet passenger's seat, behind the driver's bench.

A rigid canvas roof protected us from the summer sun, but the sides were open, allowing in billows of dust and grit from the roads. It was a carriage that could be used only in warmer months, for there was no protection from freezing rain, snow, or icy blasts of wind.

Foley loaded my trunks of clothing. I'd also brought a heavy wooden chest for my study materials, watercolors, and needlework. In September the school closed for a month. Our only other days off during the year were a few at Christmastime. I hoped to discover what had happened to Charlie well before our annual vacation. But I had no way of knowing how long I would need to remain at home to get to the bottom of these mysterious doings.

We took off at a furious pace. So jostled and bruised was I by the rutted dirt roads, there was no chance of sleep. I tried to pass the time working at my embroidery. I had yet to finish little Becky's mourning picture, which I would frame and mount on the parlor wall beside Papa's. But the bumps and jounces made me keep sticking myself with the needle and I finally had to put my work away.

It was nearly the end of the next day by the time the carriage reached the new Baltimore-Washington toll road. I was glad to see the pebbly macadamized highway stretching out straight and true, a dark gray line cutting through brilliant green farmlands south from the city dwellings of Baltimore. At last, I released my grip on the seat and napped without continually bashing my head against the carriage roof.

When I awoke it was dark, and I brought out a hard green pear and the remaining butter-bread Mrs.

Brown had packed for the trip. "Would you have some, Foley?" I asked, leaning forward on my seat to offer him half my bread. I hadn't seen him eat as much as a mouthful of food since we'd left Philadelphia.

"Nay," he replied as sullenly as if I'd offered him a clod of dirt for his meal.

Since he seemed so rude and unfriendly, I ate everything myself without remorse.

We had stopped only to rest the horse and relieve ourselves. I napped as I could while Foley drove on, very slowly now as it was a cloudy night and the road was hard to see without moonlight. It was beginning to get dark when I opened my eyes again. I looked forward to the driver's seat. Foley sat as stiff and silent as ever, his gaze straight ahead on the road. I recalled overhearing Mr. Black, the stable master, telling Cook about the boy.

Foley—I knew not his familiar name—had been brought from Ireland by my grandfather. He was an indentured servant, which meant he had been purchased by Grandpapa by paying off his family's debts and providing the boy with passage to America. In turn, Foley would work for our family for an agreed upon number of years, without wages, but he was clothed and given food and a straw bed in the stables. He would be made a free man after the term of his contract ran out. That might be three years or seven, or more. This was unlike the situation with slaves, who remained a family's property until they were sold or they died.

Although I sometimes wondered about the unfairness of human beings being owned like horses or land, it was the way things had been since long before I was born. My parents and grandparents had always kept servants—some free, some indentured, others bought as slaves. I generally gave it little thought. But when I did I felt an unpleasant pinching feeling in my stomach, so I tried not to think about it.

But back to Foley . . . more than these few overheard facts, I knew little of him. I guessed from his beardless face and youthful bearing he could be no more than four or five years older than me; certainly he was less than twenty years old. His usual tasks were brushing and feeding my grandfather's horses and shoveling out their stalls. Even at the distance between our seats, he smelled of horse dung. Old Salem, a man of color, usually did the driving, but lately he'd become confused about directions and distances. Mama feared Salem might lose his way if he traveled too far from the house on unfamiliar roads.

But Salem at least talked to me while he was driving. Rides never seemed long with him at the reins. Foley hadn't spoken more than five words since we'd left Philadelphia, the day before, even though I had asked him a few questions to elicit polite conversation. I finally decided such a dull-witted servant wasn't bright enough to understand my mission, so I said nothing of Charlie, the letter, or my suspicions, and I slept.

☆ MORE TROUBLE ☆

AT MORNING'S FIRST LIGHT, THE CARRIAGE RUMBLED up the final hill through the woods and I glimpsed the tall white columns of the main house at Elk Ridge. Tobacco and wheat fields arranged themselves like emerald- and gold-colored quilt patches around the clusters of barns, sheds, and stables.

Men and women, both white- and dark-skinned, were working in the already hot summer sun between the rows of tobacco, slashing at the wide green leaves with enormous knives, bundling them for drying in the long, sweet-smelling sheds south of the house. Later, the dried leaves would be rolled into enormous bales, called hogsheads, rolled down to the docks by the river, and shipped to other countries. The carriage turned into the tree-lined drive that led to the house's graceful portico, and I suddenly felt overjoyed to be home.

A familiar bay stallion stood at the foot of the granite steps that rose to the front door. It looked like the horse Dr. Macaphee rode. He was a gentleman from Virginia who sometimes stopped to call while on business trips between Alexandria, Baltimore, and Washington City.

"The doctor is here?" I asked Foley. Macaphee wasn't a medical doctor. Mama said he was just called "doctor" as a courtesy because he was a learned man who had once taught at a college in New England.

"Sure and he is, miss," Foley agreed in a thick Irish brogue.

He climbed down from the carriage to tie the horse to an iron hitching post. Turning around, he held out a hand to help me down from the carriage.

"Had Dr. Macaphee already arrived when you left to fetch me?" I asked.

It wasn't unusual for travelers to stay for weeks while visiting family or friends, since any sort of journey was hard and long. And overnight stops at a friend's home were far more pleasant than a stay in one of the many roadside inns that offered only the crudest accommodations. Because Elk Ridge rested almost exactly midway between Washington City and Baltimore, Grandpapa often found himself taking in road-weary guests—some, he barely knew.

"Foley?" I repeated when he didn't immediately answer me.

"Ah now, I'd say he's been here a good week, anyway."

"A week?"

"To help the missus through these difficult times, says Cook."

"Oh." I suddenly realized that, although *I* didn't believe Charlie was dead, Mama *would.* Completely.

She hadn't wanted my brother to go to sea in the first place. As if the usual dangers of storms and a war weren't reason enough to avoid sailing on ships, there was the impressment of our sailors by both the British and the French.

Papa had tried for years to appease Charlie's fascination with the sea. Finally, he had told Charlie, "I will apprentice you to a Baltimore sail maker. At least then you can be close to the docks and to the ships that anchor at Fell's Point."

I think both my parents believed Charlie would soon learn to hate the damp, slimy wharves and the vulgar men who worked there. Then he'd give up his dream.

But I knew Charlie better.

After Papa died, my brother again pestered Mama to let him go to sea, and she, not having the strength or heart for argument, at last relented. "You may sign on with a merchant ship as cabin boy," she said with a resigned sigh, "but only if both captain and vessel are recommended to me by someone I trust."

Barely two weeks later, Dr. Macaphee told her of an old friend, the captain of a merchant vessel, whose own son was Charlie's age. Captain Zachariah Moses, of the *Liberty*, would be happy to educate her son in the profession of the sea, and protect him.

Charlie was thrilled.

Mama was reassured, but only for a few weeks. Then we discovered Captain Moses was no longer trading in tobacco, flour, cotton, and East Indian spices. He'd recently discovered privateering to be far more profitable.

Mama was shaking, pale, and weeping at the news. I'd never seen her so distressed. "I withdraw my permission for you to sail on the *Liberty*," she told my brother.

But Charlie calmly reminded her of what Papa had often said: "Without privateers, America will lose the war. We have only a few dozen ships in our navy, against Britain's royal fleet of hundreds."

My mother, hearing her son speak her dead husband's words, simply gave up the fight. In the end, my fourteen-year-old brother went to war, not because of our family's patriotism, but because my mother had been worn down by death, illness, and mourning.

Now, as I hurried up the steps and onto the wide veranda, I pressed my hand over the thick packet inside my cloak: Charlie's letters. He had written to me every week he'd been away, posting his messages whenever his ship made port. I had read their thrilling words dozens of times—to myself by candlelight in my bed at night, to Amelia or any of the other girls who would listen by day. How I had yearned to share his adventures. To feel the salty sting on my cheeks and the rocking of the deck under my feet! But as the war grew more and more bloody, I feared for Charlie's life. How awful it would be if he were struck down by cannon fire or mortally wounded in a sword battle.

I glanced impatiently over my shoulder and down the steps at Foley. Tapping my foot, adjusting my skirts, which were hopelessly crushed from the journey, I waited for him to catch up and open the door for me. But he was still unstrapping my bags from the carriage, moving as sluggishly as a bat in daylight, and apparently no one inside the house had noticed our arrival.

A body might wait forever for servants! I thought irritably. Flinging open the door, I ran inside.

I stood quietly by myself for a moment, enjoying

the safe feeling of being home again. The foyer was lined with ceiling-high mirrors, making the narrow hallway that ran from front to back of the house appear endless. White wooden paneling covered the ceiling. The floor was cut from squares of pink Italian marble.

I ached to run upstairs to my very own room, but first I had to find my mother. "Mama," I called out, but not too loudly in case she was napping. "I'm home."

There was no answer.

I glanced toward the gently curving stairs that led to the second floor. A line of formal oil portraits followed them upward, proving to visitors we were a wealthy family—for only the rich could afford decoration for their walls. Many of the paintings were very old; Grandpapa had brought them from Belgium, fearing they'd be stolen by Napoléon's soldiers. Other paintings—like the one Mama, Charlie, Rebecca, and I had posed for in our garden on Congress Street—had been painted recently in America. That one was my favorite.

Above the first landing was the one Charlie liked best—a picture of James Madison, our president, as a young man. He and Papa had met at college in New Jersey and only then discovered they were distantly related. They had remained close friends until Papa's death.

Young Mr. Madison's face was thin and pasty-white against a dark green background. Bright, bird-like eyes peered down the staircase at me, seeming to follow my steps. His dark hair had already begun creeping back from his forehead, giving him a wide expanse of forehead and a look of great intelligence. From waistcoat to breeches, he wore all black, as was still his habit.

The portrait made him look scholarly and tidy and serious. It didn't reveal how small a man he was. The last time I'd seen him, Papa was still alive. Mr. Madison had been only a few inches taller than I and was noticeably shorter than Charlie. I'd guess he weighed barely one hundred pounds, if that.

His enemies, and even some of his friends, called him "Little Jemmy" behind his back. I thought them incredibly rude. How tall or physically strong a person was, or what he looked like, didn't seem to me to have anything to do with whether or not he could lead his country through a war.

Hushed voices interrupted my thoughts. They seemed to be coming from the salon on my right. I turned away from the staircase and followed them into the lofty, powder-blue room.

At first there seemed to be no one there, and I stopped halfway into the room, puzzled because I had expected to find people to go with the voices. Three brass candelabra supplied little light to the room. The untrimmed wicks of their candles blew sooty trails into the air, leaving the room gloomy and cast with shadows as I peered around me. Facing each other in front of the white-marble fireplace was a pair of eggshell-damask chaise longues—fancy but uncomfortable benches meant for reclining.

On one lay Mama. Her arm partly covered her face as if to block glaring sunlight from the tall windows, even though there was none. Dr. Macaphee knelt beside her, speaking to her in a low voice.

I moved forward hesitantly, terrified that the fever might have returned after all. The doctor's head shot up at the sound of my footfall. Thick russet brows bunched together over the wide bridge of his nose. "Caroline! I didn't hear the carriage on the drive." He smiled, his lips lifting in welcome before he turned back to Mama. "My dear, you see. Your daughter has come and is safe." His head bobbed up again. "Your mother was worried that foul weather or Foley's reckless driving might have endangered your journey."

I ran to Mama as she lifted herself with a soft groan onto one elbow. We hugged tightly for a long while. When I finally pulled away to look into her face, I saw that her eyes were red-rimmed, and deep wrinkles creased her brow. But a stylish satin turban covered all but a few tight brown curls across her forehead, as if she'd made an effort to dress for my arrival.

"Oh, Carrie . . . dear girl, sweet girl. You *are* well, aren't you?" she whispered, clutching me all the more frantically to her again.

"I'm fine, Mama," I said, at last sitting up straight. "I'm sorry you were worried for me. The trip went well."

"Foley drove cautiously?"

"He was very careful," I assured her, although my bruises might have argued otherwise.

"Good. He's only eighteen and seems duller than a hitching post. But I had no one else to spare."

"Foley and I barely spoke. His eyes never left the road," I assured her, anxious to address more important matters. I took a deep breath, holding tightly to Mama's hands, feeling my heart pound in my chest. At last I would be able to ask the questions that had been gnawing like wharf rats at my insides for days. "Please," I began, "tell me everything you know about what happened to Charlie that night."

Her eyes widened for an instant. A violent tremble rushed through her, ending in her fingertips, still clasped in mine. "I told you . . . in the letter," she choked out the words.

"You told me the little that someone told you," I said. "But much of it doesn't make sense. Charlie, of all people, couldn't just fall off a ship. There must be more to this."

Dr. Macaphee made a huffing sound and thumped away from us in his hard-heeled Wellingtons. He stopped in front of the tall window and looked through it toward the woods. "Death rarely makes sense, my dear Caroline. Someday you'll understand that the best we, the living, can do . . . is deal with it."

"I can't deal with my brother's death until I understand how it happened," I explained, then repeated my reasons for thinking my brother might still be alive. They gave me the same sad, blank look Amelia had given me. I didn't give up. "Mama, in your letter you said there were people who tried to help him, witnesses to what happened."

"Yes . . . yes, I believe that's what the captain said when he came to give me the news," she responded weakly, her eyes misting and growing distant.

"They saw him fall and knew where he went under, but couldn't reach a line to him?"

"Oh." She shook her head, looking confused. "I suppose that's probably what happened. The captain didn't go into details. You see, I was so very distraught."

"Doesn't it seem strange then that they didn't find his body?"

"I don't want to talk about this," she said, covering

her ears like a child not wanting to be lectured.

"But we must find out. Don't you see?" I insisted. "If Charlie suddenly went missing, maybe they just *assumed* he'd fallen overboard and drowned. They might not have looked for any other explanation for his disappearance."

Mama pulled her hands free and shot to her feet. Her cheeks flushed a bright pink. Her eyes flashed with new hope. "Oh, Lawrence, do you hear that? There *is* that chance!"

Dr. Macaphee raced across the room, glaring at me from under his thick brows. "How can you concoct such nonsense, Caroline? You are distressing your poor mother."

"I'm not trying to upset her," I protested. "If you'll let me explain . . ."

Mama's eyes skipped in confusion between me and the doctor. She clutched at her filmy gauze skirts, kneading the fabric until it bunched and wrinkled in her fists. "The captain himself," she whispered, her words rasping in her throat, "he told me that my sweet Charles had fallen from the deck of his ship during the night and drowned. Wouldn't he have made sure of his facts before—"

"If everyone is so sure Charlie drowned in a harbor crowded with boats and seamen, someone must have found his body," I pointed out. *"Where is it?"*

☆ A PROMISE ☆

MAMA SHUDDERED, CLOSED HER EYES, THEN teetered perilously.

"Caroline!" Macaphee shouted, glowering at me as he caught her arm and gently lowered her onto the chaise. "Your imagination has taken you too far this time, girl."

"I'm all right. I'm all right," Mama murmured. "It's just so distressing not knowing what has happened to my boy. Not knowing if he is dead or alive."

I reached out to take her hand to comfort her.

"Come with me, Caroline," Macaphee grumbled. "Leave your mother to rest."

"But she needs me! She—"

Grasping my wrist, he pulled me from the room, across the hallway, and into Grandpapa's library. We were inside with the door closed before I could manage another word of protest.

The doctor released his grip and planted himself between me and the door. "I am sorry, my dear. I have no right to interfere in your family's concerns. But your mother has suffered desperately in the past year. We all must be brave for her sake. We must do our best to make this latest tragedy easier for her to bear."

"Not talking about what happened won't help Charlie," I stated.

He looked dismayed. "My dear, *nothing* can help your brother now. Can't you understand that much? The boy drowned in the harbor two weeks ago—"

"But we don't *know* that!" I shouted, my voice trembling, my face hot with frustration, anger, and helplessness. "There's no real proof of his death. So why is nobody searching for him?"

Macaphee's moss-gray eyes looked troubled. "There is a war going on, dear girl. Our ships are being attacked at sea and on the Great Lakes by a foreign navy. Men are dying by the score every day. It will be as if America had never existed, if Madison loses this war. Do you suppose one lad more or less is going to matter to a port full of sailors?"

I glared at him, not wanting his chilling words to make sense, although they did. My friends gave little thought to politics. But I had spent many exciting hours crouched outside my father's library, listening through the heavy oak door as he discussed the war against Britain with important men like Henry Clay and John Quincy Adams.

And Mama and I had visited Mrs. Madison at the president's house in Washington City. Because we were family, we were always welcome at Dolley's weekly levees. While drinking tea and munching sweet cakes, I sometimes overheard bits of the men's conversation as they passed down the hallway to the president's library. They spoke in grim whispers of bloody attacks on American farmers and their families by the British and their native Indian allies across the Canadian border. It was clear the British would destroy us, one way or another, if they could.

"Charlie may not matter to you," I muttered bitterly, "but he is my brother, and I love him."

Macaphee closed his eyes for a moment and bit down on his puffy pink bottom lip. The worry lines across his forehead looked strained nearly to breaking. I suppose I was trying his patience, but I couldn't give up so easily. I knew Charlie would feel the same if I were missing.

"I *am* sorry, Caroline," he said at last. "I shouldn't have spoken so frankly. I have hardened myself against the cruelties of death, but you are only a child. How can I expect you to comprehend what many adults fail to understand?"

He shook his head, looking so dejected I felt sorry I'd shouted at him. He was, after all, just trying to protect Mama from more pain.

"I only want to know the fate of my brother," I whispered. "I want the truth."

"That is natural," he agreed. With a sigh, he

rested a kind hand on my shoulder. "But I fear we'll never discover what we most wish for. I would give all I own to see your brother alive. In a way, I feel responsible. Captain Moses was my friend, and he promised he would keep close watch on the boy."

"Well, he obviously didn't watch very carefully *that* night!"

He sighed again. "Believe me, I'd spare your mother such grief if I were able." He shrugged wearily. "I still believe the boy could have been in no safer hands than with Captain Moses, but what does that matter now? What's done is done."

"It matters to me," I said dully. "I want evidence either that my brother lives or he is indeed dead. And if he lives, we must find him immediately, for he must be in desperate straits!"

"Your time will be better spent consoling your mother," Macaphee said. "A piece of advice: Don't ask your mother questions she can't answer. They will only upset her the more." He withdrew his hand from my shoulder and faced me again, looking dourly down his wide, pockmarked nose. "Your mother is very near breaking, my girl. After losing your father, baby sister, and brother, you don't wish to lose her, too. Do you?"

I swallowed over a raw spot in my throat and blinked at him, fighting back tears. "No," I whispered hoarsely. "I promise, I won't do anything else to upset her."

But, I thought as he nodded and turned to leave the room, that doesn't mean I am giving up.

☆ BALTIMORE ☆

I HAD PROMISED DR. MACAPHEE I WOULDN'T bother Mama with questions about Charlie's death. But neither of us had said anything about talking to other people.

Early the next morning, I found Foley in the stable behind the house. He was sitting on a tin bucket, his lap full of wet bridles, his hands covered in dirty, thick lather.

"I should like to drive to Baltimore today," I stated. "You will take me."

His head remained bowed over his work, shaggy

dark hair falling over his eyes as he continued scrubbing. A long row of harnesses he'd already finished hung drying from wooden pegs in front of him. The leather smelled pleasantly of the oil he'd worked into it after the cleaning. The pungent aromas of horse sweat and droppings and the sweet, clean straw made me think of Grandpapa, who often spent more time in his stables than in the house.

"Do you hear me, Foley?" I said. "I require transport. Nothing too large; there will just be the two of us. The phaeton will do."

"Ah, but miss, there's been na word from the big house on that." The boy stood up and put his back to me, as if to end the conversation.

I decided he must be even more stupid than I'd at first thought. When Grandpapa had purchased his indenture in Ireland, he'd gotten a poor deal indeed.

I propped my fists on my hips and scowled up at the stable boy. He was at least two heads taller than I and broad of shoulder, although the rest of him was as thin as an ash sapling.

"I'm telling you, I will go to Baltimore. I am to

make purchases for my mother, who is too ill to travel," I added, feeling foolish for explaining myself to a servant. And even then I'd been forced to lie.

He scraped a fleck of dried mud from the leather with his grimy thumbnail. "Wouldna want t' get myself in a bad way with the missus," he grumbled.

"What trouble can there be from doing as you're told?"

"As much work to do as Job before sunset, have I." He nodded toward the racks of saddles and trappings, their silver ornaments dull under layers of dust. "Master Black will ha' me hide if it ain't done proper."

Mr. Black was in charge of the stable boys and field hands. I'd often heard him bellowing at them, and seen them scattering for cover at his approach. He was reported to have a heavy hand with a whip. I had never liked his hard look, but he did keep the stables and yard in good order.

"I'll tell him I need you today," I said. "You can do this any old time."

Foley turned his head toward me. His eyes glinted defiantly for an instant before returning to their normal lackluster blue. "When do ya want t' leave?" he asked, looking away again.

"Within the hour," I told him, trying to sound fully in charge of the situation. "Bring the carriage around to the front of the house as quickly as possible."

He nodded reluctantly but said nothing more.

As I walked back toward the house, I felt a little guilty for taking Foley from work he'd need to do another day, doubled up with new chores. But it seemed to me he'd welcome a day away from the smelly stables and Mr. Black. I told myself I was doing him a favor.

Then another thought occurred to me as I crossed the dusty yard. I wondered if Foley might have heard anything about Charlie's fate. News spread through the countryside in strange ways, servants sometimes passing information from one plantation to another by mysterious means.

I decided I would find an opportune time during our trip to question the stable lad. But first I would leave a note for Mama, telling her I was spending the day with my cousins at Riversdale. Another fib, but it would save her worry.

After my father's and baby sister's deaths, when we'd moved permanently to Elk Ridge, Mama and I had taken the trouble to drive into Baltimore only once, even though we could travel on the most modern and comfortable roads available. We were more likely to travel in the opposite direction. The families we called upon socially—like the Calverts at Riversdale—lived to the south of us, closer to the capital city.

On earlier visits to friends in Washington City, before Papa fell ill, I had met Mr. George Washington, but not until after he had left the presidency. I was very young then, and he had seemed ancient to me. His white hair was sparse, and his skin looked paper-thin, showing all the blue veins underneath, like trails of ink. But his cheeks, I remember, were a healthy pink from the sun . . . and when he smiled, his eyes danced merrily. Papa was a Democratic-Republican and very active in politics. He knew all of our presidents. But his favorite, of course, was James Madison, his old friend, who had single-handedly written our Constitution. Papa had called him a brilliant man and often seized Mrs. Madison's Wednesday levees as an excuse to drive us into Washington for a visit.

I adored Mrs. Madison. Her friends called her Dolley—maybe because she was as plump and pretty as a doll. She hugged and laughed a lot, and always made me feel welcome.

The gentlemen's talk of the war with its perilous battles between immense sailing ships fascinated me, but the ladies' gossip of family scandals and comparisons of the price of lace and pewter and porcelain interested me not at all. So when the gentlemen retired from the drawing room to discuss politics and I was left with the women, I turned my attention to the delicious foods arranged on silver trays. Iced creams were one of Dolley's favorites, and I have to admit they were delicious. Rich vanilla bean, peach sweetened with honey, and cinnamon-rum—all freshly made in Dolley's summer kitchen.

There were also crisp, ripe apples and pears in season from nearby orchards, chocolate bonbons from Holland, huge Virginia-grown pecans and almonds, gooey-sweet dates and cane sugar sticks from the West Indies, as well as buttery tea cakes and homemade jams.

As Foley turned the carriage north onto the crunching macadamized highway, the sun fell burningly hot upon us and I soon wished for one of Mrs. Madison's iced creams right there and then. However, nothing but farmland and forest followed either side of the road, and I doubted I would find any chilled delights as fine as hers on a Baltimore dock—although there would be plenty else to see and eat.

Twice every year, while we'd lived in Philadelphia, Mama and I had made the trip to the port of Baltimore to purchase bolts of beautiful silks, brocades, and linens, panels of pretty spotted and flowered velvets, painted gauzes, and other piece goods to be sewn into clothing by our seamstress. Mama selected handworked Belgian lace collars, carved ivory buttons, silk handkerchiefs, plates and bowls of Nankin blue stone china, brass candlesticks, and fine damask tablecloths.

Ships by the score sailed into the harbor and unloaded their precious cargoes from all over the world. The prices were best, Mama insisted, if we haggled with merchants right down on the docks, before they incurred the cost of land transportation, which was dear.

Papa often scolded her, saying our expeditions were unnecessary and possibly dangerous. But he never forbade them, because Mama loved to test her wits against the local dealers. I shared her love of bargaining. Those trips were great adventures. We always drove away from the waterfront exhausted but glowing with victory, our carriage top-heavy with lovely treasures the ladies of Philadelphia and Washington City would envy for months.

So I was familiar with the area of the harbor from our shopping skirmishes. I felt confident I could find my way around the docks.

Foley seemed to know the route well enough, although the horse might have found Baltimore as easily on its own from habit, for Grandpapa Streck often did business there. The trip required three hours at a good trot. I gave Foley a silver half dime to pay at each toll station. It was expensive to travel on the highway, costing a full dollar to make the entire trip. But risking a broken axle on rutted local roads wasn't worth the saving.

As we left farmland behind and entered the city, the streets seemed far busier, dirtier, and noisier than I remembered. Carts, wagons, riders on horseback, and people on foot dashed everywhere in a wild frenzy, sending up choking clouds of dust.

"Why are so many people here today?" I shouted at Foley.

He shrugged and stared straight ahead, as if anything other than the horse's rump was of no concern to him.

I glared at the back of his head.

He must have felt my anger. At last, he said, "A body with any sense will be storin' up flour, coffee and tea, sugar, and beer. If the Brits attack the city—"

"Do you really think they'd dare?" I shouted above the rising clatter of horses' hooves, vendors' cries, and groaning wagons.

"Sure, and don't ya know it. Why'd ya think they blocked off the bay months ago?" Foley asked.

"To punish us. So that fancy goods from France, Germany, and the Far East couldn't get through."

"That, too, well enough," he said. "But 'tis also t' keep American ships from sailing out and restocking their cannon shot. And so's the British won't find a fleet o' privateers aiming cannon at their backsides when they open fire on the city."

"I should think if they were to attack anyplace, Washington would be first," I said. "That's where Congress meets."

Foley shook his head. "Aye, but the British hate Baltimore more than Washington City—by rights of the nuisance our privateers ha' been t' them."

I studied the ragged line of dark hair at the back of Foley's neck and realized with surprise that I'd never really looked at him. Not looked and seen him in other than a vague, shadowy sort of way, as one does with most servants. Neither had I heard him say more than a few words at a time, and those always in reply to a command. I had pegged him as brainless, but it seemed he knew more than I about the war. Perhaps he wasn't as addle-brained as I'd assumed.

Then another thought wheedled its way into my head. I was thirteen years old, and he was nearly a man. Yet *he* had to do as *I* told him. I did not enjoy following directions from the school mistresses at Madam Grelaud's. I wondered if he disliked taking orders from a girl, Mama, or Mr. Black—even though that was his pledged duty, by the piece of paper that bound him to our family. I felt a sudden jolt of sympathy for the lad.

As we entered the crowded market district, Foley steered the carriage east, then south toward the docks. We passed along Prince Street, through swarms of vendors crying out their wares or services. We passed carts and stalls piled high with ripe tomatoes, yellow and green squash, and corn, as well as peaches, nuts, barrels of flour and sugar, piece goods, tools, flower bulbs, and pottery. The blockade hadn't kept bountiful goods from Baltimore's tables.

The familiar sounds of the street market reminded me of happier trips.

"Porgies and rocks! Porgies and rocks!" cried the fish vendor.

"Scissors to grind! Razors and knives. Sharp and

ri-I-I-ight!" called a man from behind a stone wheel.

"Sweet and fat! Sweet and fat! Ra-a-a-a-aspberries, hee-ah!" a woman under a parasol sang out.

"Oysters! Raw and sweet—slip down yer gullet."

"Peanuts, roasted pe-e-e-a-nuts hot!"

The city air smelled of mouthwatering, exotic foods but also of less pleasant odors: rancid salt brine, rotting fish heads, sour human bodies, and animal dung. Our horse's hooves clop-clopped against the cobblestones of the busy streets, through puddles of fetid garbage. Puddles I'd find difficult to avoid with my long skirts, once I was on foot. I was glad I'd chosen to wear one of my older dresses.

I had planned to question Foley about Charlie as we drove. But a warning voice from inside my head had stopped me. I was afraid he might tell me something awful that would rob me of all hope. For it seemed no one other than I thought there was any chance my brother was still alive.

But if I didn't explain my plan to Foley, I now realized, he might interfere when I tried to speak to anyone but a shop owner.

"You've heard about my brother?" I shouted over the mayhem all around us.

"Aye and sure, miss."

"What do you think?"

His shoulders tightened a notch. "'Tis a great loss for the missus t' bear."

I slid across my seat to observe his face from a better angle. He continued to look straight ahead, showing me only the line of his jaw and one blue-black, beady eye, much like those of the gulls overhead.

"But do you *believe* it?" I asked urgently.

His brow furrowed. "Why should I not be believin'?"

"Because I don't. Because it makes no sense, knowing Charlie. He couldn't simply fall off the deck of a ship in port."

"Ah well, there's that," he admitted, but then closed his lips.

"No one will agree it's impossible for Charlie to have drowned."

"Not impossible," Foley corrected me. "Only improbable. You are right there, miss."

I squinted at him. For the second time today, he

didn't sound stupid. He was talking as if he'd already given Charlie's disappearance some thought.

"The reason I've come to Baltimore is not to make purchases," I admitted. "I wish to talk to sailors from Charlie's ship, the *Liberty*."

His scowl deepened and the visible eye glimmered darkly like a bonfire seen from a great distance at night. "I'll be wagerin' your ma won't want ya walkin' the docks alone, conversin' with common sailors."

"I'm not alone. *You* are with me."

"No."

"No, what?"

"I'll be stayin' with the carriage and horse," Foley stated. "They are my responsibility."

"What about me? Whose responsibility am *I*?"

"Your own, I'd venture," he pronounced between gritted teeth, turning away so that I could no longer see even the one side of his face. "Since ya took it upon yourself t' prevaricate t' me regardin' your reasons for comin' here."

I thrust myself back against the hard leather seat and glowered angrily at his rigid spine. I had deceived him, that was true. But it had been for a good cause. Leaning forward again, I whispered at his ear, "If I tell you *everything,* you must come with me."

"And have your grandfather's mare and new carriage stolen?" He laughed. "Na likely, miss."

I had a feeling he was calling my bluff. He was clever enough to realize what would happen if anyone at Elk Ridge discovered he'd allowed me to go off in the city on my own. Mr. Black would surely give him a fearsome beating.

"You would rather return to Elk Ridge alone," I whispered sweetly, "and report that you've lost your mistress's only surviving child?"

His shoulders slumped and, muttering to himself, he glared at the torn knees of his breeches. I could tell I had won. "We shall have t' pay t' have the mare watched," he pointed out after he'd done cursing under his breath.

"I have money!" I said triumphantly.

☆ THE DANGEROUS DOCKS ☆

FOLEY BARGAINED WITH A FARRIER, WHO AGREED TO lct us leave the carriage and mare in his shed while we walked the docks. Half his fee was paid immediately; the rest would be given him on our return.

"That worked out rather well," I said, feeling pleased with my plan thus far, although we hadn't yet begun our search.

"We'll be needin' t' move smart now," Foley said, "if we are t' return t' Elk Ridge before dark. No later than five o'clock can we be departin' the city."

"That only gives us four hours, or a little more.

Maybe, after all, we should split up," I suggested hopefully. "I will be careful and I promise I won't tell a soul that you let me out of your sight."

"Not very likely, miss," he snapped.

"Why not?"

"T'would be far too dangerous. A young woman like you, alone in a place like this?" He snorted and shifted his feet nervously. "Likely to attract the wrong kind of attention."

I grinned, tuning out his warning but enjoying the words he'd chosen. "A young woman," he'd called me. Is that how he saw me? I felt twice as grown up now.

We began walking south, along the busiest wharf. The summer sun was blisteringly hot, and I wished I'd thought to bring my parasol. Shoppers, merchants, and roustabouts rushed from here to there—carrying parcels, loading or unloading flatbedded market wagons and two-wheeled carts, shouting down a recent arrival to town for news of the British. At the end of one pier, a horde of people pushed and shoved for a look at a wooden billboard on which had been listed wares to be auctioned later that same day.

Now I could see ships anchored in the harbor—brigantines, barks, flatboats, frigates, scows, and sloops. The boats strained and creaked in a sad chorus as the waters rose and fell, rose and fell, as if they were impatient to be away from their moorings.

"Excuse me, sir," I said, stepping up to a sailor who had paused to light his pipe. "Would you be aboard the *Liberty*?"

"Naw, miss. Not I," he muttered, squinting at me through thick puffs of smoke.

"Do you know any of her crew?" I asked.

He shook his head. "Heard of her, but can't say when I last see'd her, if I ever did."

"Thank you, anyway," I said politely, then turned to Foley. "Let's try that group of men over there." I pointed out three more sailors standing in front of a saloon.

"As ya say, miss," he muttered without enthusiasm.

The next hour was hot and disappointing. We plodded up and down the docks under the merciless sun, but failed to find a single crew member of the *Liberty*. Although several seamen recognized the name of the schooner, only a few had actually seen her. And of those there were none who could be sure they had done so in recent weeks. Not one sailor could tell us her current anchorage, although it had to be somewhere among the ships crammed into the main harbor, or just to the north at Fell's Point.

But I was determined not to give up. The filthy saloons lining the waterfront left much fertile ground for us to till. I felt sure one of these foul-smelling, greasy establishments would present us with a knowledgeable source.

At the outset of our queries, Foley had warned me about the natural state of sailors when confined to land—that being stumbling drunkenness. Foley was right: Even the more temperate among them seemed to have imbibed a good pint of rum by midday. The air was thick with the stench of the dark island brew and of corn whiskey. Their answers to our questions were often incoherently slurred or interrupted by sudden, incomprehensible laughter. Why they should think our questions humorous was beyond me.

"I suppose they have nothing better to do than

drink while waiting out the blockade," I commented.

Foley hid a smile and glanced shyly at a female nearby who was dressed garishly and reeked of cheap perfume. She seemed (like other women I'd observed strolling the docks) to know every man who passed her. She had a smile, saucy wink, and cheerful comment for each of them. I quickly seized Foley's hand and led him away when he looked as if he might stop to talk with her. We had no time for making new friends.

We questioned several more sailors and dock-hands as we walked, but they claimed to know little more about the *Liberty* and her crew than we already had learned: The ship was a privateer with a reputation for success.

After several tedious, unproductive hours, we came upon yet another cluster of seamen, seated on stacks of splintery planks at the end of a pier. They were playing cards on a dirty faro cloth thrown over a crate.

"Wait." Foley stuck out his arm to block me. "We'll be tryin' somethin' different this time, I'm thinkin'."

"What?"

"Ya stay here. I will go alone t' talk t' them."

I glared at him. How dare he order me about as if *I* were the servant? "Why shouldn't I go, too?" I demanded.

"If there be rumors 'bout your brother's death, they'll talk t' someone like me before someone like you," he said flatly.

My mouth fell open at his cutting tone. But he might be right, I thought. If sailors were anything like servants, they would share their sly gossip only with one another.

"Ya wait here," he said. "Just far enough so's they don't know you're with me."

I stepped behind a tall coil of hemp rope, each rough strand as thick as my arm. Foley approached the faro players.

They glanced up at him furtively but didn't object to his peering over their shoulders at their hands. After two deals, one of the men spoke to him, and Foley nodded solemnly, then added a few words of his own, none of which I could hear. Two of the sailors exchanged cryptic glances. One laughed, shaking his head as if at a joke.

Foley laughed, too, then said something more. I tried to shut out all other sounds around me, straining to hear their words, but failed.

Overhead in the sun's merciless glare, seagulls cried out eerily, warning off hungry rivals as they wheeled through the salty air. They eyed a fishmonger's growing mound of fish heads with greedy, black-button eyes. A boy tossed a bucket of trash fish and scraps in the gutter at my feet, bringing the birds down in a thrashing, screaming cloud. The stench was horrid. I covered my nose and mouth with one hand and dashed hastily away.

At last Foley bid the cardplayers farewell and casually strolled on as he'd come. He gave a low wave, signaling me to meet him at the next corner. I leaped forward, eager to hear what he'd discovered. But something unexpectedly held me back.

Looking down, I saw a huge, hair-covered hand curled around my arm.

I cried out, trying to pull away, but the fingers were terribly strong and swung me around to face my captor. An old man with tobacco-stained whiskers, scabby-red face, and rummy breath stared into my eyes from inches away. "Wha's yer name, hon?" he slurred, yellow spittle dribbling from one corner of his pulpy lips. He squinted as if to keep me in focus.

"It's no business of yours!" I shouted, gasping at his foul stench.

As old and bent as he appeared, he was remarkably powerful. He blinked at me through jaundiced eyes, paying no heed to my struggles. A black wool cap was pulled low over his ears and forehead. I couldn't have said whether he possessed thick shanks of hair or none at all.

"Let me go!" I demanded. "My . . . my brother's coming back any moment. See, he's just over there. He'll whip you for daring to touch me!" But Foley, I saw with increasing horror, was walking away along the wharf, apparently unaware of my peril.

"Yer brudder?" the grotesque fellow mumbled, sounding confused.

"Foley, stop!" I shouted. "Help me! Foley!"

The stable boy turned around and stared in my direction, but didn't move toward us.

The old man blinked, then blinked again. At last he released my arm. Backing away and muttering to himself, he quickly hobbled around a corner and was gone.

Foley was grinning as he casually strolled back to meet me. "Found a chum, did ya?"

I shivered. "He was a loathsome old wharf rat. Do they never bathe? What took you so long?" I snapped at him, trying to disguise how truly frightened I had been.

He looked amused. "Told ya, sure I did, this were na place for a young female alone."

I sighed. As long as he spoke about me as if I were a grown-up lady, I decided I could allow him almost any shortcoming as a servant. "What did you find out?" I asked, straightening my rumpled sleeves where the dirty old creature had pawed them. "Or were you merely swapping bawdy stories with those sailors?"

"Walk this way." He lowered his voice when I fell into step beside him. "I'm not swearin' what I heard is of any import. But it's clear we're wastin' our time in Baltimore. I'm drivin' ya home now, miss. I'll explain on the way."

I grabbed the rough muslin of his shirt. "No! Tell

me here . . . *now*! There might be a clue we should follow while we're still in the city."

"It's fixin' t' storm," he said stubbornly, scowling at muddy clouds mounting overhead. "She'll be gettin' dark early. I've got me work t' do."

"I don't care. Tell me." I stomped my foot at him. *"I order you to tell me this instant!"*

His black eyes blazed fiercely down at me, his hands clenched into tight fists at his sides. I thought for a moment he would strike me, though if anyone saw him it might well cost his life.

Without another word, Foley turned and marched away, heels digging into the weathered planks with shuddering *whump-whump-whumps*. I feared I'd made him so angry, he might leave me to find my own way home. Feeling a score of sailors' liquor-glazed eyes fixed upon me, I looked around nervously. Would the loathsome creature who had seized me moments earlier come back if he saw me unaccompanied and defenseless? Was he hidden in the crowd, waiting his chance to grab me?

"Foley!" I cried.

☆ ONE CLUE ☆

"I'M SORRY, FOLEY!" I CALLED OUT, RUNNING AFTER him. "I didn't mean to offend you!"

He kept on going, his long legs taking such enormous strides I feared I wouldn't be able to catch up with him before he reached the farrier's shed. I lifted my skirts—now stained and mucky with dock gloop—and ran faster, skidding over spongy planks, bumping into startled tradespeople, lurching carts, and cursing seamen. At last I was beside Foley and we were rushing through the crowd together. His face was a fiery red, his eyes ablaze with anger.

His arms pumped like steam engines at his sides.

"Please, I didn't mean anything bad by what I said. You were laughing with the sailors. What was so funny? Were they merely swapping drinking stories, or was something awful mentioned about Charlie? Why did you say we should leave now?" I wiped at drops of sweat rolling down my brow, for it was still blisteringly hot, although the sun was sinking lower in the sky. I was trying to be patient, knowing I'd hurt the stable boy's feelings, though I couldn't say how. After all, *he* was the one in the wrong. A mistress had every right to demand loyalty and an honest answer from her servant.

He didn't slow down until we were less than a dozen steps from the farrier's shed. I believe it was only because he was winded from his crazed dash along the docks that he stopped.

"Foley, he's my brother," I pleaded. "If he were yours, would you give him up for dead so easily?"

"'Tis no information ya can use, miss. Only crude rumors and confusin' hearsay." He jammed his fists down on his hips and drew a single deep breath, then stood tall, scowling across the harbor at Fort McHenry on the far shore.

I followed his gaze. A brilliant tricolored flag flapped from its ramparts as if taunting the British navy. Fifteen bright red and gleaming white stripes, one for each state in our Union. Fifteen white stars against a field of blue, representing the thirteen original colonies plus Vermont and Kentucky, which had joined our country after the Revolution.

"'Tis not important," he murmured, his eyes still fixed on the American flag.

"I'll decide what is or is not important," I stated.

"Hard ta believe that lad was your own flesh and blood," Foley remarked. "He seemed a cautious and levelheaded boy."

"And I am, too! I mean, not that I'm a boy, of course," I added quickly, blushing at the amused expression on Foley's face. "But I'm very careful most of the time. I just need every piece of information I can get! Please," I pleaded reluctantly. It didn't seem right to be begging a servant for his help, but if that was the only way to get it . . .

He shifted his gaze to three men in stylish waistcoats and expensive-looking hats who stood nearby. They had been talking but now were silently watching us. I guessed that Foley was worried my shouting would cause them to interfere on my behalf, believing I was unable to handle my disobedient servant.

Foley motioned me toward the far side of the wharf, then dipped his head and spoke into my ear. "Two of those old faro-playin' sea dogs reacted immediate when I spoke of a lad drownin' in the harbor."

"I thought I saw them looking slyly at each other!" I cried triumphantly. Something of great portent was about to be revealed to me, I was sure.

"Then another o' the sailors said he heard rumor of the *Liberty* runnin' the blockade only days afore. How she escaped, none of 'em seemed to be knowin'—but apparently 'tis not unheard of for a schooner or one of our other faster ships to sneak 'tween British boats under cover o' darkness on a moonless night."

Foley paused for a moment. This time I didn't push him but let him take his time. This was valuable news indeed!

He continued, keeping his voice low. "A bristly faced man with a crippled hand recalled the fifteenth bein' calm. The first mate of another ship agreed, sayin' he himself had been on a ship in the harbor near the *Liberty,* and it was so still all through the night that his own ship couldn't ha' filled a sail to move out t' open sea even if the Brits had allowed it."

"Not exactly the type of weather that throws a sailor off a deck!" I cried. Here was news I could welcome.

Foley held up a hand before I could express my joy. "But others couldn't agree on the weather," he continued. "They recalled the night as havin' a hearty breeze, bringin' up whitecaps even in the sheltered harbor." My heart sank. "And," he continued, "none of them remembered an alarm goin' up as would happen if someone fell overboard. But come mornin' there was talk of a missin' cabin boy."

"What does all of this mean?" I asked, dismayed at the jumble of reports.

"It means," he said calmly, digging his boot heel into a soggy board as he wiped drops of sweat from his upper lip on his sleeve, "as time passes, facts tend t' get muddled in people's heads. We are still without proof of your brother's death or survival. We are wastin' our time here."

"No!" I shouted, forgetting the people nearby. "It means someone is *lying*. The captain claimed that while the *Liberty* was in the harbor, my brother fell into the water and crew members tried to save him. But nearby ships heard nothing of his distress. And now his ship has somehow escaped the British blockade, where scores of others cannot. Does all of this not sound odd to you?"

Foley scowled at his worn shoe tops. "Odd, perhaps, but it helps us not at all."

Nevertheless, my heart pounded wildly in my chest. Lies meant deceit and guilt. Guilt meant blame. But was finding someone to *blame* for Charlie's death what I really wanted? No. What I yearned for was proof it had never happened. I wanted to know without question or doubt that my brother was alive.

Foley narrowed his dark eyes and scanned the brackish water crowded with ships—their bare masts stark against the blue sky. Garbage and driftwood floated about, clunking noisily against their wooden hulls. When he looked back at me, his expression was solemn. "Why would the captain lie?" he asked.

"I don't know yet. That's what we must find out," I argued urgently.

He shook his head. "You'll be searchin' for treachery where there's none, Miss Caroline. You're wantin' t' believe your brother is still alive. So you conjure up stories in your head, refusin' t' pay attention t' what we've learnt."

He sounded disgustingly like Amelia. I turned my back on him. I heard Foley sigh in frustration, but still refused to look at him.

"If you'll be wantin' t' talk with any more of these smelly old wretches, we'd best be doin' it now," he said reluctantly. "Your mother will worry if dark falls and ya haven't returned."

"Yes," I agreed, relieved that he had decided to humor me. I nodded toward a splintery sign hanging over a saloon door. "The Gilt Goose—I think we missed that one."

Sadly, by the time our allotted hours were up, we

knew no more about my brother's fate than we had after speaking to the faro players.

In the days that followed our Baltimore trip I dwelt upon the one fact we'd discovered that seemed sure: At some time after Charlie's disappearance, the *Liberty* had run the British blockade and was now outside the harbor. But that information only left me hungering for more. I wondered if my brother's fate and the covert movement of the ship he'd been on were connected in any way. I couldn't yet see how, but then so little made sense.

I agreed with Foley that there seemed to be no reason for the captain to lie. In fact, he appeared a resourceful seaman who knew his duty and had performed it better than most. It was a privateer's job to evade, harass, or attack British vessels wherever and however possible. Blockade runners were heroes to all Americans except the British sympathizers who were against the war and wanted America to rejoin England.

But every bone in my body ached with suspicion that there were wicked secrets surrounding Charlie's disappearance. Days later I was still trying to invent an excuse to return to Baltimore, convinced that there lay my best chance, maybe my only chance, of gathering more clues. But Mama wanted me near her all the time and found scores of duties to keep me in the house. When we finished the chores Mama had planned for one day, there was still the endless needlework—embroidering table and bed linens, Rebecca's unfinished mourning picture, initials and tatting to be added to purchased handkerchiefs. Never could I find a spare moment.

I assisted her in packing Grandpapa's framed paintings from the stairwell and parlor, in case we were forced to flee Elk Ridge when the British army landed. Then we spent two more days polishing silver spoons, forks, knives, and tea service, because she claimed the servants didn't do a careful enough job and might steal valuable pieces when she wasn't watching them. Another day we made candles of beeswax—a smelly and disgusting job that I hated above all the rest. I hoped to take a long walk before supper to clear the awful stench from my nostrils so that I might face food.

As we worked over the steaming vats, I wished with all my soul that Dr. Macaphee would return to occupy Mama's time, so she would take less notice of me. But he had ridden off in haste three days earlier, and she didn't seem to know when he'd return from his business in Virginia.

Later that day, I asked Mama to repeat Captain Moses's exact words when he'd come with his tragic news.

"Oh, Caroline . . . must I?" Her cheeks drained of all color, and her eyes became glassy and distant.

I remembered the doctor's warning. "Never mind," I said quickly. "It's not important." And I returned to knotting strands of wick to a long stick, spacing them carefully so the dripping icicles of wax wouldn't bump into one another and ruin their smooth shapes.

At last I grew so bored with our work, I sat at the heavy trestle table in the kitchen and stared out the window. "The gladioli are beautiful," I said, pointing to the garden Mama had planted with tubers and bulbs the previous spring.

"Yes, they are. Your grandfather sent them along

with tulips and irises from Brussels," she said wistfully. "We should write to him asking for more bulbs to plant along the other end of the house." She sighed and gazed out the window. "Unfortunately, there is no telling if any mail is getting through these days. I wrote to him about Charlie, but whether or not he received my letter . . ." She sighed again.

I followed her sorrowful gaze through the window and thought I saw movement among the cluster of black locust and willow trees bordering the creek. But when I looked back at her face, it was expressionless. If anything had been there—a deer or fox or some other creature—she wouldn't have been cheered by it.

She drew a shuddering breath and turned away from the window. "I want to speak to you about the other day, Caroline. About your visit with Emma."

Emma. My cousin, the one I was supposed to have called on when Foley and I took the phaeton into Baltimore.

"Yes?" I said, my heart hammering in my chest. Had the stable boy betrayed me? The villain! I knew he wasn't to be trusted.

I faced the window, my hands clutching the sill. I didn't want her to see my face, because Mama had always been able to read my thoughts so easily. Suddenly, stepping from behind a thick-barked poplar a little way from the woods, there appeared a woman. She was wrapped in a tattered, dark brown cloak—almost the exact color of tree bark. She stooped and plucked something from the tall grass between the trees, then stooped and plucked again, adding to a small bundle cradled in her left arm.

I frowned, wondering who she might be. She wasn't well enough attired to be anything but a servant, but she wasn't employed at Elk Ridge, and no other house stood within three miles.

I felt a pressure on my shoulder and became aware of Mama's voice, as if from afar. I turned back to face her. "Did you hear me, Caroline?" She squeezed my shoulder again.

"I—no, I'm sorry."

"Emma's mother called on me yesterday, while you were out walking. When I remarked that you seemed to have enjoyed your day at Riversdale, she informed me that you hadn't been there."

"Oh," I said.

"Where were you, Caroline?"

A hollow feeling settled in my stomach. My tongue felt thick, hot, awkward in my mouth. "Baltimore," I admitted, unable to lie while she stared searchingly into my eyes. "I asked Foley to drive me to Baltimore."

"To shop?" she asked. "Why didn't you tell me you wanted to—"

"No, I . . . the harbor—"

Her expression changed from perplexed to annoyed. "You had to go to *that place* and see for yourself," she said, her voice quivering like Amelia's tuning fork.

"Oh, Mama!" I groaned. "I'm sorry. But there must be more to what happened to Charlie than the little we've been told. Dr. Macaphee says I shouldn't speak of Charlie in front of you, but I'm sure something isn't right. You know how he loved the water, how he respected and understood it like no one else."

Her hand was quaking violently. She withdrew it from my shoulder. "I remember," she said, her eyes drifting away. "The doctor means well. He believes he is protecting me. It's not your speaking about Charlie's fate that pains me, Caroline. It's holding out hope. This wound in my heart . . . if I let it remain open, it will never heal."

She pressed her fist to her chest and held it there, as if trying to stop her very life breath from escaping. Again, she captured my eyes with hers. "Please try to understand, daughter. There is no evidence of Charlie's survival. Without that, all the questions and prayers in the world are useless. I cannot continue to hope . . . cannot bear to imagine him walking into this house ever again."

Tears trickled down her cheeks. She wept silently, making no attempt to wipe away the dampness. The sorrowful blue-green of her eyes reminded me of the ocean. Her breath whispered in and out of her body like a sea surge. "We must accept God's will," she murmured at last.

"No," I said, just as quietly as she, but with a firmness that sounded like an echo of my father's voice. "I will know the entire story of Charlie's death. Or I will find him alive."

Lifting her hand from her breast, she covered her eyes with both palms. "Do what you must. But I forbid you to leave Elk Ridge alone again."

"I wasn't alone. Foley—"

"Is a servant. He has work to do, and is not suitable as a young female's traveling companion. I only sent him the once to Philadelphia because there was no one else to fetch you from school."

"But I must—"

"Silence!" Her hands fell limply from her eyes, which were swollen and red with tears. Straightening her shoulders, she stood erect as she pulled a lace handkerchief from her sleeve and blotted her eyes. "I'm not being cruel, Caroline, so do stop glaring at me. There have been British scouting parties and rumors of raids into the mouth of the Patapsco River only a few miles from here. I will not have you wandering about unprotected. Am I understood?"

"Yes," I whispered.

"You will remain here, at Elk Ridge."

"Yes," I repeated. But in my heart, I couldn't say if I'd be able to keep this promise any better than my others.

As I turned away from her, I glanced once more through the windowpane. The woman in brown had disappeared. But the woods were thick, and I wondered if she was still there, somewhere, watching me peer out at her. How had she come to be here, and for what reason?

I feared I was beginning to imagine puzzles and mayhem in every situation and person.

☆ DOLLEY'S LEVEE ☆

DURING THE NEXT FEW DAYS, MAMA, THANKFULLY, found fewer chores for me to do. But having more time to myself only frustrated me the more.

What news of Charlie could I possibly unearth while I was confined to Elk Ridge? I constantly dwelt on images of the faro players, of sailors and barkeeps and dockside roustabouts I hadn't had time to question, whose tongues might tell valuable secrets. Even the friendly, painted females who had attracted Foley's attention might be able to tell me something—since they seemed to know so many of the seamen. I desperately needed to find a way to reach the world outside Elk Ridge. But I could see none.

One afternoon when I felt especially glum, Mama sat beside me on the front steps and put an arm around me. "Young women spend their whole lives at home, keeping their houses in order. This is no surprise to you, Caroline. Why do you think it should be otherwise for you, dear girl?"

I shrugged.

"Would you like for me to read to you?" she asked.

"I learned to read for myself years ago," I said bitterly.

"We might go for a walk," she offered.

"I've already walked every inch of this prison," I replied.

If Papa had been alive, I would have been punished for speaking so disrespectfully to my mother. But he wasn't. And, although I'll admit to being ashamed for being so rude to her, I also sensed some measure of freedom might be gained if I let her know how angry and frustrated I felt. Hadn't Charlie eventually badgered her into letting him sign on with the *Liberty*?

Then why shouldn't I succeed in pressing my own case?

Yet I dared not speak of Charlie as my reason for needing freedom to move about. It was clear the doctor was right in one matter: Mama's heart was in a terribly frail state. The simple mention of Charlie's name by anyone in the household brought a sickly pallor to her cheeks and tears to her eyes, just as now.

"Caroline, I know you miss Charlie." She stood up and rearranged her skirts. "And I know you wish he were back here with us."

I swallowed with difficulty and folded my hands on my knees. "Yes."

"I haven't done very well myself, dealing with his loss. Perhaps it's time you and I tried to move on with our lives."

I looked up at her and frowned. I didn't like the sound of this. Move on? What drastic measure was she contemplating? "What do you mean?" I asked.

"You used to enjoy accompanying me to Mrs. Madison's levees. Perhaps we should go again, as we used to. Try to be around other people and not shut ourselves off so."

"But the war . . . you said it was unsafe for me to ride about with the British so soon to land."

"Alone, it would be, of course. But we shall travel with the protection of two of our stable lads, and Dr. Macaphee assures me we will have ample warning before a full-scale landing—at least enough to return to Elk Ridge and gather our belongings, if we must leave for safer quarters."

I didn't understand how the doctor could be sure we'd be a jump ahead of the British army, but I didn't want to discourage her from the trip, since she seemed to be looking forward to it. I also wondered if it might not prove useful to my cause.

"What do you say, my darling daughter?" She was working hard at being cheerful. Her eyes were too bright, her voice too light. "Shall we live a bit dangerously and seek out our old friends for comfort and companionship? We've worked terribly hard these weeks. I think we deserve a taste of Dolley's luscious iced creams, don't you?"

Her smile was weak but tender. I couldn't hold on to my anger any longer, and I truly wanted to do something to make her happy.

Leaping up from my stone seat, I hugged her hard. "Yes, Mama, I think we should go."

I eagerly looked forward to Wednesday and our trip into Washington City. Dolley's guests would include women of influence from Maryland, Virginia, and even more distant parts of our country who were visiting the capital. Any one of them might know something of Charlie, or suggest a method of searching out the truth that I hadn't yet explored. If I had been furious for being kept at home in the past weeks, now I was quite beside myself with anticipation.

Mama must have sensed the cause of my soaring spirits, for on the day of the levee, as Old Salem turned our carriage into the familiar curving drive that led to the president's house, she took my hand in hers and entreated me with her eyes. "Caroline, I hope you'll enjoy yourself, but do limit your conversation to polite social matters. This is not a time to speak of your fantasies concerning your brother."

My stomach clenched. "But Mama, Charlie's disappearance is all that matters to me. Whatever shall I talk about if not that?"

"Dolley's jam cakes," she said firmly. "Or the ladies' dresses."

"Such silly chitchat," I fumed.

She squeezed my hands with a hint of her old firmness. "You are not allowed to bring up the subject. Is that understood?" She paused, waiting for my answer. "If you can't give me your promise, we shall return to Elk Ridge this instant."

My heart sank. "Yes, Mama."

She sighed, looking relieved, then released my hands as the carriage rolled to a stop. "People need moments to escape their troubles," she murmured softly. "Cousin Dolley will undoubtedly wish to keep conversation light with the war so close at hand."

The bitter taste of failure filled my mouth. I fervently wished I were older—free to make my own decisions, free to go wherever I chose. Thirteen was a terrible age! Even Foley, in his indentured status, sometimes seemed to have more freedom than I.

Mama proceeded up the steps of the president's house, and I followed disconsolately behind her. I had lost all enthusiasm for the day. Time was running out. Before long, the British would be upon us and we might be forced to flee Elk Ridge. The safest place to go would be to the west, away from the coast where they would land their troops. The farther I was from Baltimore, the more impossible it would be to learn the truth about Charlie. If, by the slimmest chance, he was still alive and in need of our help, he would never receive it.

I curtsied politely to Mrs. Madison when she greeted us just inside the door. She wore an Empire-style gown with lace ruffles at her wrists and a satin turban over her curls. As she hugged Mama, she cast me a quick, warm smile over her shoulder. I chose not to linger as she murmured condolences over our family's tragedies.

Moving toward the drawing room, I found it already crowded with guests. Trays of delectable treats and two silver tea services sat on tables at opposite ends of the sunny room.

I looked around the room, abuzz with women and their daughters in fine dresses of the latest Continental styles, hoping to find someone my own age. Cora Adams and Becky Fields were whispering together in one corner. But they were two years older than I and talked of nothing but the suitors who came calling on them, or the cost of their imported gowns and slippers. If they had overheard any news of a privateer ship or Charlie, they would not have bothered to recall it.

I made my way through several smaller rooms, wandering with no particular purpose, idly observing the carefully matched furnishings and the paintings on the walls. One was of George Washington, looking somewhat younger than when I had met him. I wondered what would happen to all of these lovely things should the British actually fight their way past our soldiers to attack Washington.

Without considering my direction, I turned into another room. When I looked up, I could see it very much resembled Grandpapa Streck's library. Leather-bound volumes were arranged in tidy rows on shelves to my right. I pulled one down and, with indifference, read the title imprinted on the spine in gold letters.

"Why the pinched puss, miss?" a wispy-thin voice asked from behind.

I whipped around to find a small gentleman in a black waistcoat sitting at a modest cherry-wood desk. Both man and furnishing were so unremarkable, they had escaped my attention.

"Oh," I said, "pardon me. I thought the room empty, sir."

When he stood, it was then I recognized him. He was only as tall as I. His meager frame seemed barely to support his dark apparel. Only a white shirt collar relieved the starkness of his costume and attracted any light to his pallid complexion.

I hadn't seen him since the day he had taken the oath of office. President James Madison smiled at me and said, "So the gossiping old biddies have frightened you off, too?"

"No, sir," I said, curtsying quickly. "I just wanted to be alone for a while."

"A young girl and parties . . ." He attempted a smile, but the effort of contorting his face only made him look more nervous. "One might think a perfect match—but not for Caroline Dorsey?"

"No, sir," I repeated politely.

"Can't say I blame you. I'm not much at ease with strangers myself." His reedy voice suited his frail build. Mr. Madison reminded me of a timid field mouse that, suddenly discovering itself inside a grand house, has no idea which way to scurry. But his eyes were sharp and intelligent, and a gentle curve still tugged hopefully at his lips.

"I'm sorry I've disturbed you," I murmured. "You must be very busy."

He nodded but made no move to return to his desk or escort me from the room. "I have heard, of course, of your family's misfortunes, Caroline. Your father . . . he was a friend. A good and loyal friend. I will miss him."

"I shall miss him, too," I said over a sudden tightness in my throat.

"And your little sister, gone also to fever. And your brother . . . I'm not sure I heard the particulars. It is a sad business, nonetheless, losing loved ones. And this being a time of war makes it all the harder to bear, I'm sure."

I wished he'd stop. My eyes were burning, and I couldn't let our president, of all people, see me weak and weeping. But he seemed unaware of his words' effect on me. His glance drifted sadly to a tall window as if he could see the British fleet closing in on our shores, even from where he stood.

He must have felt as helpless as I, but for different reasons. A year ago, I'd overheard Papa talking to his friends in Philadelphia about the sad state of the American army. They'd had difficulty finding recruits, and for those loyal few the army did enlist, there was little time for training and almost no money for weapons. With such a small and poorly equipped army to fight thousands of professionally trained and well-armed British soldiers, the defense of most cities and towns would fall to individual citizens and local militias—composed of farmers, bakers, blacksmiths . . . ordinary people.

"War," he whispered, as if his thoughts mirrored mine.

"There are those who say this is our second war of independence," I said. I was not breaking Mama's rule against speaking of serious subjects, since Mr. Madison had brought them up. I felt sorry for him. He had tried so hard to employ reason before war. But those stubborn Englishmen wanted to control us, as if we Americans were still part of their grand empire. Thus we were at war again, defending our freedom only a few decades after the Revolution.

"Truly, it is," he agreed. "The days to come will decide America's fate. I pray we survive our trial."

"If we lose, will we fall under the king's rule again?" I asked.

"Yes." He nodded sharply, then faced me again. "Do you know, Caroline, I've always thought of war as a chess match, as a gentleman's game. I have never witnessed an actual battle, you see. But my generals tell me it is nothing like a game at all. It looks now as if I will soon see for myself."

I recalled how Papa had often worried over the

fate of our president and the men sitting in Congress, should the war be lost. "Will the British shoot you if they capture you?" I asked.

His thoughtful expression didn't change. "Perhaps. It may be I will deserve death if I fail to wrench America from this infernal struggle with England."

"My brother is just fourteen!" The words exploded from my lips before I could stop them. "*He* doesn't deserve to die."

Mr. Madison sighed. "I'm so sorry, my dear child. I understand he was a cabin boy on a privateer."

"He was on a schooner, the *Liberty*." I quickly told him all Mama had heard from Captain Moses of the night my brother had disappeared. After that I described my trip to Baltimore and the conflicting information we'd discovered there.

"Sir, you can see there are things about my brother's disappearance that fail to make sense. I wonder if you could help me investigate this mystery," I said, suddenly inspired. "Perhaps you might appoint someone to look into the facts?" I stared pleadingly at him, unsure what powers, if any, he could use on our behalf.

Mr. Madison slowly shook his head. Outlined against the towering, sunlit window frame of his office, he looked so very fragile. I tried to imagine him seated on a horse, leading an army into battle, bellowing orders at his men . . . but couldn't.

"I am sorry, Caroline." His voice was so gentle, I had to strain to hear the words. "I regret the pain you and your mother have suffered. But I cannot spare a single man to search out the information you need."

"Surely just one person—"

He shook his head again. "Times are desperate. Every man, woman, and child will have a job to do in the days that approach, if our country is to be saved. Should your brother be alive, he will come to light in time. If not"—his blue eyes dimmed with sorrow—"if not, Caroline, he will think no less of you for mourning him while you do what you can for your country and family."

My mouth tasted salty, as if the tears I had been willing from my eyes had taken another route, down the back of my throat. "What can I do?" I asked.

"Stay at your mother's side and support her."

I let my glance fall to the floor, unable to hide my

disappointment. "Yes, sir." There was, I knew, nothing more to be said. Mr. Madison was repeating Dr. Macaphee's lecture, but in gentler words—one boy's life mattered little when the survival of an entire country was at stake. Feeling selfish and unworthy of help, I turned to leave the room.

A bashful cough made me stop and look back at the president.

"I can do one very small thing for you and your brother," he said.

"Yes?"

"I shall tell your story to others. I shall mention your brother's name, the *Liberty,* and Captain Moses to my generals and advisers if the situation allows. I shall ask them to spread the word as they can. It may be that some fact will come to light."

My heart soared with hope. No one before had believed that Charlie might still live. I wanted to throw my arms around our good president but held myself in restraint. "Thank you," I said politely.

"If I do hear anything, good or ill," he promised, "I will send word to you at Elk Ridge."

☆ THE LETTER ☆

IN THE DAYS THAT FOLLOWED, I PRAYED FOR NEWS from Mr. Madison. Sadly, none came. I soon was as determined as ever to return to Baltimore. There, I was still convinced, I would find more answers than anywhere else.

Locating the *Liberty* and questioning her crew would have provided the most valuable information. But the privateer, having cleared the blockade, had to be far out to sea by now. She might be almost anywhere in the Atlantic Ocean. Some privateers ventured into the Caribbean. Others crossed the Atlantic and lurked in the English Channel, harassing British shipping to the Continent.

However, it seemed possible that other American ships might have seen her and have word of her. If I could find a sailor from another blockade runner, he might give me more current information on the *Liberty*'s whereabouts. I might even be able to convince a crewman, for a fee, to deliver a letter to Captain Moses, requesting additional facts and details about Charlie's last days aboard his ship.

I had recently learned from Foley, who seemed less reluctant to talk with me since our journey to Baltimore together, that many of the ships set small boats and crew ashore at secret beaches to obtain necessary supplies. "I was told by a traveling brick maker," he reported, "that the eastern shore of Maryland still isn't completely under British control. Citizens risk their lives by supplyin' privateers with sugar, flour, bacon, fruits, and vegetables, as well as gunpowder and shot for their cannon."

"So," I said thoughtfully, "that might be one way to contact ships, by leaving word at a privateer's store."

"Might be at that," he agreed.

"How do ships get their mail?" I asked.

"'Tis on these same beaches, if it's na too dangerous t' let it be known ahead of time when they'll be puttin' ashore. Should the British find a privateer's beach, they'll wait on 'em and take the crew by surprise. But I've heard mail is also sometimes swapped between ships at sea."

My conversation with Foley gave me a new idea. I retreated to my room, took quill and ink in hand, and composed a letter to Captain Moses.

After finishing it, I then copied off three more sets of the same message. From what I'd learned of seamen on the Baltimore docks, I suspected their natural laziness might outweigh their not-so-natural honesty. Once paid for his delivery service, a sailor might well drink his fee and toss my envelope into the harbor, knowing he'd never see me again. By sending four copies of my letter, chances of one reaching the captain would improve.

If Moses was the honest and caring man Dr. Macaphee had originally believed him to be, the captain would answer my letter, explaining in detail the happenings of the night of July fifteenth. If he had something to hide, he probably wouldn't respond at all. But I would be no more in the dark than I was now.

The next step was locating the most promising carriers for my letters, which probably meant leaving Elk Ridge. The likelihood of seamen wandering up to our door was slight.

Another week passed with no chance at all of my traveling anywhere. Although Mama seemed to enjoy our day with Mrs. Madison, she had been frightened by talk among Dolley's guests, who were already removing their families to safer places in the countryside. Mama set to her own preparations with renewed energy. She kept the servants busy helping her cover and crate furniture, vases, and dishes. Carpets were rolled and tied with heavy cord. Shiny silver cutlery and bowls were laid in folds of damask tablecloths, then rolled up inside them and packed into trunks.

Meanwhile, I took advantage of her distraction to sneak off from the house and sit on the fence overlooking the toll road, where I could watch passersby.

The trickle of citizens fleeing Baltimore became a steady flow of entire families, taking with them all they could carry in grand carriages, rickety wagons, or packed on the back of a mule.

I shouted to people as they plodded by, asking their destinations. I would have given out my letters to any who agreed to carry them toward a port, but they were all traveling in the wrong direction.

"Is every citizen of Baltimore leaving her to the British?" I asked.

"Nay," an old man said. "There are many who stay behind to protect their property or join the militias."

Another man heard him and stopped to talk. "I'll be going back there in another day or so, after I've made the family safe at my brother's farm." He pointed to his wife and three children in a cart, jostling up the road. "The Virginia militias have put out a call to arms. They'll stop the Redcoats long before they reach Baltimore, they will."

The next day, a woman told me she'd heard the British had landed somewhere in Virginia, but others said their fleet was still a good way offshore, sending in only small advance parties to determine where they should put their troops ashore. I could hear the tension in people's voices. No one knew what might happen next, but all feared the worst.

At last "the good doctor," as Mama called Macaphee, returned to us.

"I was gone far longer than I'd hoped," he told us that night over a supper of ham, new potatoes, and summer peas. "There was so much to do."

I listened intently to his descriptions of travel on horseback along the Virginia coast, then north again, toward Washington City. I was hungry for any news to cheer us.

"Have the British landed?" Mama asked worriedly. "We hear so many different rumors."

"I assure you, I saw no sign of them in my journeys. But it is only a matter of time, I fear. And when they do come, I worry that the king's agents will seize the banks in Baltimore and Washington, and with them all of our assets." He leveled a solemn look at Mama as he chewed his meat. "That is why I have removed my bonds and cash money to a safer location." He pointed the tines of his fork at Mama. "You should do the same, Margaret. I will be glad to assist in any way you wish."

"It's not the money I worry about. Are *we* safe here?" Mama asked. "I have been working the servants day and night, preparing to evacuate, if necessary. But I would do anything to avoid leaving this house."

The doctor looked sad. "It is difficult to say, dear lady. Who knows what the British have in mind for us?"

Who knows indeed, I thought dismally.

Macaphee stayed for three days, then a letter arrived by messenger and he rushed through the house in a state of agitation. He ordered his horse brought around from the stables and told Mama he had unexpected financial preparations to make. "Are you sure you do not wish me to withdraw your accounts, too?" he asked her. "This may be the last chance you'll have."

"Oh . . . I don't know." She bit down on her bottom lip and blinked at him in confusion. "I don't want to act hastily. It's not only my husband's estate I worry about. My father's, too, must be decided. I wish there was some way I could consult with him."

"There is too little time," he warned her. "All I need is a writ from you to make your assets safe."

"Maybe it would be a good idea," I suggested. "We can't let the British take all Grandpapa and Papa worked so hard for."

But my mother shook her head. "I can't think of money now, not when our very lives may be at risk. Please come back quickly, Lawrence," she begged him. "We need you here. You are a good friend."

"I will return soon," he promised. But he did not smile at her, and I could see how distressed he was.

As he turned to leave, I had a sudden wonderful inspiration. I rushed upstairs to my room and snatched from my writing table the packet of letters I'd written. Chasing after Macaphee, out the door and down the wide granite steps, I caught up as he was mounting his horse. "Let me come, please, sir!" I cried.

He turned in his saddle and looked down at me, one half of his bushy red brow cocked in surprise.

"Why, Caroline? It is far too dangerous for you to be on the roads."

"I need to deliver these letters, and I can do that without interrupting your business. I'll be good company," I added quickly. "You must be tired of traveling on your own for so long."

It was true—lines of exhaustion marred his face, and muddy circles underscored his eyes. He stared gravely down at me and shook his head. "This is no time for you to be rambling the countryside, missy."

Straightening up, I looked him solidly in the eye. "Mama said I couldn't leave Elk Ridge, except with a proper escort. I can't think of anyone she would trust more than you."

Slowly, his lips lifted in a smile. He seemed to relax in his saddle. "I am flattered, Caroline. But my trip will be a fast and furious one, with no time for socializing. I will be taking the back roads and riding hard . . . to avoid possible run-ins with the enemy," he added quickly. "I cannot risk your being harmed. That would destroy your mother."

There seemed to be no way to get what I wanted

without telling him my true intentions. "The truth is, sir, I must get a letter to the captain of the *Liberty.*"

"A letter?" he repeated. "Whatever for?"

A subtle tightening of his tone made me think I'd be wise to bend the truth ever so slightly. "I want to know about Charlie's last days," I said. "My brother wrote to me often. He loved being on a ship. I want to know that even his last hours were happy."

Macaphee studied my misting eyes, then looked away for a moment, focusing on the glade of tulip trees. "Yes," he said at last, "I can understand how you must feel. I have an idea."

I waited, fearful that he was going to find yet another excuse for putting me off.

"Why not let me take your letter to the *Liberty*? I will put it directly into the hands of the captain." He held out his gloved palm and, smiling, waited for me to give him an envelope.

"The ship isn't in the harbor anymore." I explained about the *Liberty* having run the blockade.

His mouth dropped open, and he looked startled. "How did you ever find that out?"

"A sailor in Baltimore," I admitted quickly, hoping he wouldn't ask for details that would get me into worse trouble with Mama.

"I see. Then getting any message to the ship will be very difficult indeed." He observed me thoughtfully. "You are quite a clever girl. Have you learned anything else about the *Liberty,* or your brother's death?"

"No," I said, "not really. But I've learned that ships sometimes meet at sea, to exchange news of the war and to trade mail. I had hoped to get a letter to the captain and that he might answer my questions by return note."

I lifted the bundle of duplicate letters I'd carefully prepared and placed them in his wide hand. "If I can't go with you, you might leave one of these with any ship's hand or sailor whose ship stands a chance of crossing paths with the *Liberty.*"

Macaphee's horse huffed and pranced impatiently, but the doctor controlled it with a sharp jerk on the reins. He studied the four envelopes. "The smaller, fleeter sloops, I should think," he murmured. "They would have the best chance of running the blockade."

I smiled. "Thank you."

Tucking my letters inside his vest, he said, "It's good to see you looking brighter again, Caroline. Now go to your mother. I'm off."

I stepped back, and Dr. Macaphee snapped his crop against the horse's rump. He galloped down the long, dirt drive toward the toll road, leaving a gritty cloud of dust to settle slowly in his wake.

☆ THE PEDDLER'S WARNING ☆

ON ONE OF THE HOTTEST DAYS OF THAT SUMMER, A peddler—his wares clanging and banging along the sides of a creaking, red-painted wagon—turned in at our gate and started toward the house. I watched him approach from my bedroom window. He was a strange sight—fat as a pregnant sow, nearly bald, sweating inside what appeared to be a heavy woolsy suit. His bright wagon lurched and heaved up the drive, pulled by a bony dapple-gray.

I rushed down to meet him, hoping for news or an answer to my letter, although only a few days had passed since Macaphee's departure. The peddler stopped at the back door to beg a cool drink and show his wares. Cook was waving him into her kitchen when I arrived.

"'Tis a murderously hot day," he complained through sun-cracked lips as he straddled a chair in the kitchen. I wondered if its rush seat would hold his substantial weight. "Come all the way from Boston, I am—originally, that is. Not accustomed to such steamy mornings."

He observed me over the lip of a tankard of cider that Cook had brought him. Before I could pose my first question to him, he asked, "Would this be the Dorsey family plantation?"

My heart leaped. I raced around the table and stood over him, nearly too excited to form intelligible words. "*I* am Caroline Dorsey!" I choked out.

He looked up at me cagily from beneath lowered lids, streaked with grime from the road. "You have concerns about a brother, I hear tell?"

I silently thanked Macaphee for a well-placed letter. He was indeed a clever man! "Yes, yes . . . my brother Charlie! Have you a response from Captain Moses?" I held out my hand expectantly.

"Don't know 'bout no responses from captains," he muttered, his Yankee accent coming through stronger as he relaxed in Cook's chair. "All I can tell you is, cross t'other side of the bay, a fella gave me a ratty piece of paper for delivery to either of the Dorsey women, south of Baltimore. Were a fortnight ago, more or less."

Now I was fully confused. How had word of our troubles reached someone on the eastern shore more than a week before Macaphee set off with my letters? "Let me see the paper!" I cried.

"Fella said I should follow the new toll road south from Bal-tee-more," he continued, pausing to take a long swallow of cider, "to a plantation set up on a hill. Cursed note has caused me nothing but bad luck."

I waited for him to pull the message from his vest. Instead, he scratched himself between his thighs, gazing pleasantly at me as if he'd forgotten what we'd been talking about.

"Where is it?" I demanded.

"Given the terrible hardships I suffered 'long the way," he said slyly, "a loyal courier might expect some small token of gratitude. Hey, miss?"

I scowled suspiciously at him. "I haven't seen any note yet."

"It's gone," the peddler admitted with a sigh. He sipped again, tilting back in the chair. "But there are—"

"Gone?!" I cried, stamping my foot on the wood planks. The table wobbled. Cook looked up disapprovingly at me from her cutting board.

"Yes," he explained calmly. "You see, after crossing the bay by flatboat with my wagon, I run into a British patrol. Now I weren't too happy about that, let me tell you. But as an honest tradesman, a civilian with no want to fight for or against anyone, I seen no reason why they should detain me. So I answered their questions straight out and calculated to soon be on my way. But the soldiers, they found that scrap of miserable paper on me."

"What difference should a letter make?" I asked.

From a corner of my eye, I saw Foley slip into the kitchen. Cook waved a towel at him as if she were shooing out a chicken that had wandered into her kitchen. But he made no move to leave.

"They thought it was written in code and I were a spy," the peddler continued, rolling his eyes dramatically. "Me—a spy! Took an entire night of convincin' to talk them out of putting me in shackles and shipping me off to bloody gaol on Tangier Island. Even so, they kept the paper, sayin' it could be in code. Can't tell you how afeared I was. A British prison ain't my idea of a—"

"You want to be paid for something you can no longer give me or prove you ever had?" I asked, astonished.

"She's right up here," the peddler said, tapping his forehead with a grimy finger. "Them words is stuck like glue."

Foley slid silently closer, his eyes narrowing. "Tell the young miss what the letter said," he snarled.

The peddler jumped, looking frightened at first, then relieved when he saw Foley's ragged attire and realized he was only a servant. "I'll want fair payment. I judge the words will be worth much to Miss Dorsey."

Without waiting for a say-so from Foley, I ran from the kitchen to my room and quickly returned with a fistful of coins. I showed them to the peddler.

His eyes gleamed greedily. He reached out.

I drew back my hand. "First, the letter's contents," I said.

The man looked at me, then at Foley, and set down his tankard on the table. Lowering his voice dramatically, he spoke. "The note, it warned of danger 'far beyond imagining but dangerously close to home.' Them's the exact words."

I frowned, confused. "But that means nothing. It's a silly riddle!"

"What else?" Foley growled. "It must have said more."

The peddler blinked at him. "And if there were, lad, it might come easier with some encouragement." He turned and looked meaningfully at me. "I do believe the sun has addled my memory."

I hastily dropped two half dimes in front of him on the table. "More, if the words are worth it," I said sharply.

He shrugged. "You be the judge, miss. The message said you and your mum best trust no one . . . but for one person."

"Who?" I demanded, sitting down to face him.

"Cain't say as I recall a name. . . ." He scratched his head, then his crotch again. I averted my eyes.

Foley lurched forward with a roar, reaching for the peddler's throat. Cook scurried from the kitchen with a shriek.

"Leave him be, Foley!" I cried, jumping between the two men before Foley could lay hands on the peddler. "I want to hear what he has to say."

"Sure and he's toyin' with ya, miss!" Foley growled, glaring dangerously at the man. "Out with it, you crook—or ye'll have na teeth t' eat the biscuits those coins will buy."

The peddler's eyes worriedly flashed from Foley's clenched fists to me. "You cain't expect me to recall a whole letter, not word for word. I don't read so well to begin with!"

"That was a *private* letter!" I cried. "You shouldn't have been reading it at all."

"Ah," he said, a foxy glint in his eyes, "but aren't you glad I did? If the soldiers had taken it off me without my knowing at least a bit of it, you'd have nothing. Now would you?"

I looked sternly at Foley, who backed away a few feet. The peddler might have been without scruples, but he was right. "Go on," I said, jingling a few coins in my cupped hand. "Remember more, earn more." If he could play that game, so could I.

The man licked his lips. His watery eyes narrowed to reptilian slits. "Something about . . . and here I cain't honestly recall the precise words . . . something about invisible enemies working against your family. Then an accident, I think it was, involving a ship."

I clutched my hands to my chest. The peddler's eyes brightened, seeing he'd hit on something important to me. I gave up two bits this time.

"Ah, yes, I remember clearer now," he continued. "The letter said this someone you could trust would find you. Meanwhile, you must be patient." He considered his words. "Yes. I think that's all. I've forgotten the rest in my terror of the British sentries." He scratched the tabletop, indicating it would be an appropriate time for the rest of the coins in gratitude for his cooperation.

I frowned, trying to make sense of his muddled message.

"What signature was affixed t' the letter?" Foley asked.

"You mean, who sent it?" The man scowled, then took another long swallow of cider. "Cain't remember that neither, sorry to say. If I should, would it be worth another few coins?"

In answer, Foley spat on the peddler's boot. I thought this terrible manners, but wished I'd thought of it first.

The man glared at Foley, then turned to me. "The one who brought me the letter was a young lad, if that helps."

I felt dizzy with hope. "A boy! How young? Do you have a name?"

The man shook his head, then abruptly stood up and glanced toward the door as if ready to leave. "Didn't give it. Cain't say why he would." He paused.

"Do you think your cook might spare a piece of cake, and maybe one of those lovely ripe pears I see in her larder, for a weary traveler who has delivered important news?"

I ignored his greedy begging. "What did the boy *look* like?"

"Oh, he was a raggedy urchin. Dirty brown hair. Walked with a terrible limp. A cripple from birth, I'd say. 'Bout yay tall." He held one hand level with his chin, which was only as high as the top of my head.

"That doesn't sound at all like Charlie." I sighed, disappointed.

But if the message hadn't been from Charlie, who had given it to the urchin to pass along to the peddler with instructions that it should come to us? Captain Moses? Was he trying to tell us, secretively, that there was more to my brother's disappearance than anyone had let on? Maybe there was a reason someone wanted Charlie dead. And what about the warning to trust nobody except one particular person—whose identity had been lost when the British took the letter? Was there also a reason to hurt *us*—Mama and me?

Although I tried to question the peddler further, he only shook his head and swore he could offer nothing more. With some coaxing from me, Cook timidly returned to the kitchen. She gave the man a pear and some butter-bread and sent him on his way.

Overcome with frustration, I trudged outside and around the house to the garden. I was too deep into my thoughts to admire the roses and spikes of sweet lavender. Foley finally caught up with me. "You all right, miss?" he asked.

I couldn't look him in the eye. I felt like such a baby for wanting to cry. "Yes." I sniffled as quietly as possible, blinking to keep my eyes dry. "Yes, I'm fine, thank you."

"I wouldn't be puttin' too much faith in that scoundrel," he said. "Where there's a penny to be made, men like that'll say or do anythin'. The devil be in 'em."

"But he *knew* our names! And he *knew* about Charlie."

"He only said somethin' concernin' an accident. Nothing about the *Liberty* or your dear brother by name. The knave could have asked down the road a piece and been told the Dorsey land was just over the rise. A field hand coulda told him as much of your family's story as anyone in the county has overheard."

"What of the warnings?"

"He wanted t' sound dramatic, to bring up your price for his news. Who knows if any of it were real."

"Oh," I said, bitterly discouraged.

"Aye." He glared at the packed red clay that wound between the flower beds, and thrust his thumbs into the waistband of his trousers. "It may all be fiddle-faddle . . . or it may be somethin' important. Remember, the note—if there ever was one—spoke t' ya of patience. Might be that's very important. Ya must be vigilant, miss, see what transpires."

"I hate waiting around and doing nothing!" I screamed, kicking my foot in the dirt. "Something must happen soon, or I shall burst!"

"Burst, is it?" he said solemnly. "Like a ripe watermelon?" He turned away to leave, but I caught a mischievous grin and muffled words. "Expect that shan't be a pretty sight, Sean me boy."

☆ A SURPRISE VISIT ☆

THAT NIGHT I LAY IN BED AWAKE. THE SCENT OF honeysuckle crept thickly through the warm September air but did nothing to soothe my anxiety. Rumbling booms in the distance made me think of cannon fire. Had the British already landed? Might their soldiers be creeping toward us along the Patapsco River, through the dark? I tried to think of pleasanter things. But nothing happy came to mind.

Instead, I dwelt on the confusing warning delivered by a greedy peddler.

Oh, Charlie, who should I trust? I thought, tossing

on my bed, kicking at the linens. The letter entrusted to the peddler, if it had ever existed, warned I should put faith in only one person. But how was I to know who that person was unless I had a name?

Certainly I could trust Mama, that was without question. Besides, the peddler had said the note was for *both* Dorsey women, so the warning applied to her as well. Cursed man and his piecemeal conundrum of a message. Cursed British for snatching the letter from him! The missing words, not those delivered, were clearly what mattered most.

And where were my own four letters to Captain Moses at this very moment? How far might they have already traveled by way of Macaphee?

Flashes of sheet lightning brilliantly ignited the black skies to the south. Long, threatening rolls of thunder grew louder as the night deepened. Thunder, not cannon fire, was what I'd heard. This time. How much longer before it was the other way round?

Knowing I wouldn't be able to sleep while my mind returned again and again to thoughts of Charlie and the war, I left my bed. Still in my cotton chemise and barefooted, I slipped down the stairs and out the back door into the garden. At this time of night, hours after dark and hours still before dawn, no one would be about—not even servants.

I walked slowly, trying to clear my mind. The skies flickered with long, jagged sabers of white light, then went dark again. A chill wind that spoke of soon-to-come autumn blew across the garden, bending the heads of the roses, whispering through the glade at the river's edge. I looked up and thought I saw a shadow move against the wind. I stood still, waited, watching. It shifted again, this time not a hundred feet away from me.

My first thought was of the strange woman I'd glimpsed at the edge of the woods. But before I had a chance to call out or move even an inch, I heard two hasty footfalls—heavy, stumbling—coming my way. Then there was silence, except for the sound of raspy breathing. The sickening-sweet odor of rum—so strong, it made my eyes water and nose twitch with distaste—assailed my nostrils.

"Mr. Black, is that you?" I demanded in my most

imposing voice of the shadowy figure. Along with wielding a quick whip, the stable master was known to enjoy his drink now and then.

There was no answer.

"Whoever you are, if you have business at this house, come back in the morning." I was no longer able to keep my voice from shaking.

"True enough," a deep voice rumbled. "Jake's got business with you, Missy Dorsey."

I fell back two steps, my heart in my throat. "Who *are* you?" I squinted, but the moon was clouded over and gave off only a watery, deceptive light. The wide form shifted, then shifted again unsteadily.

"I seen you on the pier," the gravelly voice said.

"I don't think so." I started backing away more quickly. If I cried out for Foley, would he hear me? Everyone in the main house was surely asleep. "I never go down to the river for the tobacco loading."

"Not thar, not thar," the figure grumbled. "Bawl'imer. That's where you be."

"Yes," I said slowly, still backing away as I connected the stench of the creature with another frightening meeting. "I was there. But that was weeks ago."

The yellow glow from the moon speckled the path with light as the clouds thinned. I could see the man better now. He was very large and not at all a pleasant sight.

His face was rough, with an untended beard of wiry gray hair. His eyes were enclosed in rolls of ruddy flesh. Above the beard, the cheeks were gouged and scarred with coarse lines—as if he'd spent his entire life out of doors in the worst weather. Ragged muslin garments, soiled and reeking of the foulest mixture of smells, clothed his enormous body.

"I tried to . . . to talk to you," he whispered between belches.

"No, I don't remember you," I insisted, although I did. "Go away."

"Sure, missy." To my horror, he stumbled forward three more steps, coming straight up to me. "Sure you remember Old Jake."

His hand moved with such speed, I didn't have time to react. The gnarled fingers seized my arm in a painful grip.

"Let me go!" I cried, flailing at him with my free fist. "Foley! Mr. Black, help me!"

The enormous fellow looked alarmed, as well he should have been, since we were only a few feet from the stables. If any of our people caught him hurting me, they'd beat him mercilessly. Even in his drunken slather, he must have realized his peril.

"Hey, missy, quiet," he hissed. "Shush . . . quiet down." Instead of releasing me, he drew me closer to him. I could feel the hot blast of his breath on my face. He was old, but shockingly strong, as I had already discovered. "Old Jake, he's got something for you. News you'll very well like. 'Bout yer brudder."

"News about Charlie?" I gasped incredulously. Suddenly, I was confused. Dare I risk listening to the disgusting creature? As unlikely as it seemed, could this man have some word of Charlie? Was it possible that in his pub crawls around the harbor he had discovered information we had missed? "What news?" I cried, at last breaking free of his grip.

"Yer brudder"—he began, but looked up worriedly at the sound of a stable door banging open.

"Miss Caroline!" Foley's voice split the darkness. "Is that you? What's wrong?"

I shoved the old man in the middle of his chest to regain his attention. "Tell me. What about my brother?" I must have pushed too hard. He teetered backward. Hopping to keep his balance, he awkwardly tumbled into a border of ivy. I ran forward to try to help him to his feet. "Speak, man!" I shouted at him. "Quickly!"

At the urgent sound of my voice, Foley bellowed out an alarm to the other boys.

Jake struggled to his feet with surprising speed. "They was tryin' to kill him, they was." The slapping of running feet across the yard mixed with halloos and my shouted name. The old man's eyes grew wide with fear, and he staggered away from me.

"Who was trying to kill Charlie?" I asked. *"Who?"*

"Them bloody spies!" Jake blurted, then he turned and lumbered away into the dark.

I tried to chase after him, but the fabric of my chemise tangled around my ankles, tripping me. I gathered up my foolish hems and dashed after the old sailor, but plowed into an object moving at lightning speed. Down I went onto the pebbly ground.

Someone swore loudly in an Irish brogue. I looked up in irritation, fighting to catch the breath that had been knocked out of me when I fell.

"Sure and what are ya doin' out this time of night, miss?"

"Never you mind, Foley!" I cried. "There's a man in the garden . . . heading for the woods. Stop him!"

Foley peered into the dark as a second groom arrived, his shirt flapping open, as if he'd been in bed and grabbed whatever clothing was closest to hand.

"Come on!" Foley shouted to the other boy. "We'll get the bloke."

Since there was nothing to do but wait for them to haul Jake back to the stable yard, I sat where I had fallen, in the dirt, rubbing my bruises and trying to remember how to breathe normally. Shouts of alarm, orders, and confused responses flew between the two boys in the dark. I listened for Old Jake's liquor-thickened protest, which would mark the moment of capture, but it never came.

After nearly ten minutes had passed, the yard fell

quiet again, and Foley reappeared, wheezing and coughing, moving a lot slower than when he'd left me. The younger boy trailed tiredly in his wake.

"Well?" I asked.

Foley scowled at me. "You wouldn't be imaginin' a man from shadows, miss?"

"A shadow can't grip my arm so tightly, it throbs!" I shouted up at him. Ignoring his offered hand, I scrambled to my feet. "You let him get away!"

Foley looked blankly at me. The other boy grunted in passing and continued toward the stable.

"He was the same creature who attacked me on the wharf," I informed him.

Foley frowned, then gave me a pitying look. "All this way he's come? That seems unlikely. Ya were havin' nightmares, maybe walkin' in your sleep."

"No!" I insisted. "He said his name is Jake, and he had word of Charlie." My heart pounded loudly in my ears. At last I had word that confirmed my brother was alive! "You frightened him off before he could say much," I accused. "All I got out of him was something about spies trying to kill my brother."

"Spies?" Foley repeated.

"Yes."

Foley looked doubtful but said nothing.

"Perhaps *he*, Jake, is the one person I was meant to trust." Even as I pronounced the words, they sounded ludicrous. Trust a drunken dockhand? "You know, the one the peddler told us was mentioned in the letter?" I reminded Foley.

"A letter we can't be sure ever existed," he pointed out. But Foley must have seen the new hope in my eyes, and he seemed to want to find a way to reassure me, even a little. "If it's important enough, this Jake fella will find another time and way t' reach ya."

"But what if we've frightened him off for good?" This was my darkest fear now: to have lost the single fragile link I might have had with Charlie.

Foley considered this. "True, he might be too wary of the plantation now." He shrugged. "Nothin' for it now."

I shook the dust out of my chemise and sighed as Foley walked away. "Then we must find a way to return to Baltimore," I called after him. "Soon!"

If he heard me, he didn't let on.

☆ ONE LAST CHANCE ☆

THE REMAINDER OF THAT NIGHT AND INTO EARLY morning, I was plagued by Old Jake's words. I might have agreed with Foley, that what I thought was a crazy, inebriated old man was really only an apparition or dream, a troubling memory of the filthy creature who had accosted me on the docks. But when I turned over my wrist, dark purple smudges marked where his thick fingers had bitten into the flesh, trying to hold me until he could make me listen to what he'd come to say.

Spies . . . out to kill Charlie. But who were these

spies, if they existed? And why had they singled out a simple cabin boy on a privateer?

I dressed at first light and walked outside, looking for Foley. The air smelled sweet and new. The stables were quiet, the boys just then beginning to rouse themselves to their chores. Foley, one of them told me in a half-asleep voice, was already off on an errand for Master Black and would be gone for an hour, maybe longer.

"Bother the boy," I fumed. "Taking off just when I need him."

I stood at the garden's edge and stared at the thick hedges of roses, then beyond them to the trees bordering the river. Everything looked safe and friendly in daylight. Yet I wished the night back, needing to know what the old man had come to tell me. Again, I thought about the woman I'd seen at the woods' edge, but she was nowhere in sight today, either.

While I was waiting for Mama to come down to breakfast, Dr. Macaphee, who had at last returned from his travels, joined me at the table. He looked up from his coffee and frowned. "There are dark circles beneath your eyes, Caroline. Did you not sleep well?"

His obvious concern encouraged me to relate the previous night's incident. He listened without comment, a solemn expression on his face, his lips pursed, chin propped on smooth fingertips.

"I saw this same man, Jake, when I was in Baltimore," I continued. "Then, I took him for a common sailor. He frightened me with his ramblings, and I ran. But last night, when he said those things about Charlie and spies, and a plot to kill him, I realized he might hold the key to my brother's fate!"

For a long moment after I finished, the doctor said nothing. He seemed very deep in thought. At last, he murmured, "This is very serious. Very serious, indeed. I'm thankful you weren't hurt."

"So, what do we do?" I asked, hoping he'd have an answer. "We must, of course, find this Jake and discover what he knows of Charlie. But how?"

"Rest assured, the fellow is nothing but a scoundrel. There are enough like him in the world today, taking advantage of grieving families, pretending to have knowledge of lost loved ones . . ." He sighed deeply and waved a dismissive hand. "It's an old, old trick. Don't be taken in, Caroline."

I considered his advice for a moment. He sounded like Foley talking about the peddler. "No," I said at last, "I think you're wrong. I believe the man really does know something of Charlie. And whatever it is, it must be terribly important for him to have traveled all the way from Baltimore to find me. By the way, were you successful in locating carriers for my letters?"

Macaphee swallowed the last of his coffee and patted his lips with his napkin. "Yes, but I cannot guarantee they will reach the captain. It is a very long chance, I fear, Caroline." He coughed into one hand. "Back to more immediate matters—this fellow who stalks you. An unscrupulous man with a taste for hard liquor will journey a lot farther than twenty miles for a few gold coins to quench his thirst." He studied me solemnly from beneath the red shingles of his eyebrows. "I fear this is just another unfortunate complication your returning home has created. I told your mother before that it was a bad idea to bring you home from school. And as it turns out, this is truer now than then. You've upset her more than helped her by your presence. And you've endangered yourself by seeking conversations with rogues."

I opened my mouth to protest, but he held up a silencing hand. "I don't mean that in a cruel way, Caroline. I'm simply concerned for both you and your mother. Perhaps it would be best if you returned to school now."

"But, I—"

"You will be safer there than here," he plunged on, as if I had nothing to say on the matter. "Surely this scoundrel won't follow you all the way to Philadelphia."

"But if I leave now, I may never—"

"Caroline," he interrupted. His mossy eyes locked on mine, and he leaned across the table to whisper urgently, "Be reasonable. I have word from a reliable source that the British landed at Benedict yesterday, barely thirty miles to the south of us. They are no more than three days' march from Washington, not much more from Baltimore."

"No!" I gasped, for a moment my own problems forgotten. "Will they attack Washington?"

"It seems more likely than ever now. But exactly when this will happen, no one knows." He straightened up again. "It will take them some time to set up camp and deploy their troops. Possibly Baltimore will be their first target. With the home port of the privateers burned to the ground, they may face little resistance to taking Washington City." He shook his head woefully, then looked away, and I could no longer see his expression. "I would like to see you safely away from here."

"What about Mama . . . and you . . . and all the servants? What about their safety?" Despite my occasional irritation with Foley, I wouldn't want him harmed by enemy soldiers.

"I shall suggest your mother travel inland to visit her sister in Frederick, Maryland. I will take her there myself. Things should be calmer at a distance from Washington." He sighed again. "As to the servants, we can't very well cart them all away. I shouldn't worry if I were you. The British aren't stupid. They will find ways to use reliable labor."

I swallowed and stared with no appetite at the thick rashers of bacon, fried eggs, and slabs of hearth bread with jam that Cook had put on my plate. The food had grown cold and congealed, and the sight of it turned my stomach. I pushed the plate away, not caring if I ever ate again.

I had no idea what to do, but I did know that I did not want to leave Elk Ridge. Not for Philadelphia, Frederick, or anywhere farther away from Baltimore. Let the British come, if they would. I had to find out if what Old Jake had said was true.

And if it was, if Charlie had been the target of British spies (for reasons I couldn't even guess), had they succeeded in murdering him? Or had they failed? If they'd failed, he must be alive somewhere, trying to get word to us. Was it possible that both the letter given the peddler and the message brought by rum-soaked Jake had come from Charlie himself? All along, had my brother been alive and trying to get a message to Mama and me?

But if that were so, why hadn't he come home to

us himself? Why send such inept couriers? Why not seek our help directly in eluding these ruthless spies?

I berated my own thickheadedness for not being able to unravel the mystery behind it all.

Of only one thing was I certain: If a reply arrived from Captain Moses, or Charlie tried to make contact with us after we had abandoned the plantation—we would never receive word. In the panic of war, no one from the household could be expected to put his life at risk to forward a message.

Having nothing better to do with my time until Foley returned, I offered to help Mama pack the last of the linens. Still, I dwelt on Macaphee's words . . . the crippled urchin . . . a faceless, nameless letter writer . . . the peddler, Old Jake, and that mysterious woman in the woods. All were jumbled hopelessly inside my head. I was anxious for Foley's return.

"Where are the doctor's estates?" I asked in idle conversation as Mama and I worked.

"Virginia," she replied absently. "You know that."

I nodded, supposing I'd heard him boast of his properties often enough but hadn't been sufficiently interested to remember. “Have you ever visited any of his houses?” Since I was away at school eleven months of every year, much of my mother’s day-to-day life was unknown to me, although I suspected she hadn’t often ventured from Elk Ridge since Papa’s death. “Are they larger than Elk Ridge?”

“The doctor has told me a great deal about his plantations. I’m sure his houses are as grand as they sound.” Mama placed another tablecloth in a leather-bound trunk and smoothed it lovingly, then pressed it down to make room for more.

“But you’ve not been to any?” I repeated. For some reason this point suddenly nagged at me.

“No,” she said, sounding wistful. “I know Lawrence would have gladly driven me down to Virginia to see them, if I’d asked. But I am so busy here at Elk Ridge, needing to tend to every detail of the household what with”—she hesitated, looking deeply saddened—“with all that has happened.”

She meant Papa, little Rebecca, and Charlie.

I swallowed over the acorn-size lump in my throat.

"Ah well," she continued, "I'm thankful the doctor is such a helpful man. He's been a loyal friend, a source of advice and support during these hard days."

"Yes," I agreed. But an odd notion struck me . . . one I didn't like. "Mama," I asked, "you wouldn't ever *marry* Dr. Macaphee, would you?"

She chuckled to herself, making a tsk-tsk sound she'd used for scolding Charlie or me when we were little. "No. But he has asked," she added with schoolgirl shyness, her cheeks flushing. "Caroline, you needn't worry about that. I wouldn't marry a man I don't love. And I expect it will be a very long time, if ever, before I love a man other than your father."

I wrapped my arms around her and hugged her. "I like the doctor, but not as a father," I admitted, feeling strangely relieved because I hadn't realized this possibility bothered me. I straightened up and looked at her. "He says I should return to school, that I'll be safer there."

Mama's brow puckered. "Yes, he suggested the same to me. But I told him I want you with me in Frederick."

"Oh?" I said, wondering why he had even mentioned my returning to Philadelphia when Mama had already told him she didn't like the idea. My thoughts bounced back to another, more distant conversation. "Did you give Dr. Macaphee the writ for the bank yet?"

She looked surprised at the question and shook her head. "No. I suppose it would have been the wise thing to do, in some ways. But I dare not take our family's entire fortune by coach to Frederick. What if we were stopped and robbed along the way? All would be lost. Everything." She shook her head. "I know Lawrence means well, but I would rather risk our little army holding off the British than trust myself to protecting your father's legacy from highwaymen or foreign soldiers."

I understood how she felt, but couldn't say which was the wiser course. "We will be leaving here within a day or two, won't we?" I asked tensely.

"Yes. I'm afraid so," she murmured.

"Then I will have no further chance to inquire about Charlie?"

For a moment I feared she would burst into tears

and crumple limply at my feet like a dropped table linen. But she held herself firmly upright and nodded. "I know it is important to you to learn what you can about that tragic night. But I've truly never understood why, Caroline, when facts cannot be changed." Her hand swept lightly over my head, making me feel like a little girl again. She gave me a slow, sweet, sad smile. I was spurred on by the new courage I heard in her voice and the brightness of her eyes.

"Maybe the facts don't need to change," I said, cautiously. "Maybe we need to look at them differently."

She shook her head, grabbing for a pile of linen napkins. "You're such a silly girl. Full of riddles and imagination and maddening—"

"Mama," I interrupted, "let me tell you what happened last night. Then you can decide for yourself."

She sighed but let me talk. When I finished the tale of my two encounters with Jake, relating every word he had spoken, every gesture and detail, her eyes sparkled. "He never said that these people, these spies, succeeded in killing Charlie?" she asked.

"No, just that they had tried."

"Although they *might* have succeeded."

"Yes," I said solemnly. "They might have. But *someone* has been trying to contact us, if the peddler and Old Jake are telling the truth. It could be Charlie himself."

"But surely he would come to us," she objected. How much alike we thought.

"If he could," I said gently.

Our eyes met, and I knew that she understood. One reason for Charlie to stay away was an injury so severe, he could not travel. If he wasn't already dead, he might be close to it.

"But what are we to do?" she gasped excitedly. "The British so near . . . and these messengers, we have no means of reaching them."

"I first saw Jake in Baltimore. That is where I might find him or he might find me again," I suggested.

"Now?" she whispered, fear filling her eyes. "Travel to Baltimore? With such desperation all around us?"

"It must be now, or not at all," I said. "There is still

time, while you and the servants finish preparations for leaving. If I take a carriage this very moment, I can be back before dark this day. Then, no matter how little or how much I have learned, I will go with you to Frederick without complaint . . . if that is what you want. I promise."

Mama took a deep breath and slowly let it out. Her cheeks were pale. But her eyes seemed to glow with life that had been absent since Papa's death. "I don't know why all these rumors and suppositions about Charlie being alive are beginning to sound reasonable to me. Perhaps because the alternative is too terrible to bear. Maybe we're both being foolish." She rolled her eyes and bit down on her bottom lip. "All right. You may go, but choose a dependable driver. And tell him he must come to me for a weapon to protect you both, should the need arise."

☆ IN SEARCH OF OLD JAKE ☆

"FOLEY!" I SHOUTED, RUNNING ACROSS THE YARD toward the stable the moment I saw him drive up the market wagon. "Mama says you should take me to Baltimore immediately, for tomorrow we move everything to Frederick."

He looked at me as if I were simpleminded. "Such blarney, miss, I never did hear. Mother of God, are ya tryin' t' get me in trouble again? Go away."

"I'm not lying," I insisted. "Ask Mama if you don't believe me."

He scowled at me. Accusing his mistress's daughter

of lying would not endear him to her or to Mr. Black of the heavy whip hand.

"There's no need to worry about the British," I said, my hands on my hips. "We'll be back before nightfall, and Dr. Macaphee says the British are days away."

"He is a prize, that one," Foley muttered, turning away from me to unbridle the horses.

"*You* should talk, arguing with me the way you do," I snapped. "Why must you always be so stubborn? Are all Irishmen like you?"

"They are if they know what's what—and I do." He walked one of the horses off to its stall, muttering to himself as his dark hair ruffled in the hot wind. "Phantom sailors in the night . . . brothers drowned but not dead . . . sure as the mornin' is bright, I don't know what craziness has gotten into this family. . . ."

I grinned all the way back to the house, knowing I'd won. But by the time I'd changed my clothes for the trip and we were under way in the phaeton, troubling thoughts again rumbled through my head. This time I knew who I was looking for: Jake. The question was, where to find him?

I envisioned the crowded docks, smoky saloons, dim boardinghouses, and merchants' establishments all around the harbor. Which places, I wondered, would Old Jake most likely habituate? The saloons, of course, but there must be a hundred of them in the city. Searching every one would take days.

When we finally reached the waterfront, it was as if Foley had read my mind. "It's useless, ya know," he stated in that sadly quiet Irish brogue of his, "findin' one man in a city preparin' t' battle for her life."

As crowded as it had been the last time we'd been in Baltimore, there was now not an inch of space anywhere near the harbor to park a carriage. The farrier's shed was boarded up and abandoned, as were most of the shops. Barricades of logs, planks, and shoveled dirt had been thrown up to block streets and form bunkers, behind which men could hide and fire on the attacking British soldiers. Militia crowded the streets. They sat on curbs, stood in alert, solemn groups at corners, or nervously played hands of cards on barrel tops in the hot sun.

"Nothing is ever useless, unless it's doing nothing

at all," I stated. "Find a place to leave the carriage. Please," I added when I saw a flicker of defiance in Foley's stormy blue eyes.

Reluctantly, he entrusted the horse and carriage to a boy, whom he promised a coin if both animal and vehicle were there when we returned—and a thrashing to the lad if he let them out of his sight. We started to walk as the sky darkened. Before we reached the docks, the wind had changed, blowing off the water suddenly cold. It began to rain. Hard.

Foley trudged after me, his wide-brimmed straw hat tugged low over his face to fend off the stinging torrent. I pulled up the hood of my cloak, turned my back to the wind, and walked quickly.

As we moved down the street, an awful feeling of being watched clung to my every step. I peered down side streets, but saw nothing except more men carrying muskets, rifles, and sometimes pitchforks or sticks, for lack of better weapons. They were all rushing to find shelter from the storm, far too busy to pay attention to a girl and her servant.

Foley, though with me in body, was ignoring me

in spirit. He still seemed annoyed that I'd made him drive into the city only to be met with this miserable, gray downpour. But I insisted we make use of our time. We stopped outside every open shop, house, or saloon door along the street. I asked whoever would listen about Old Jake, describing him as best I could as I shook water from my cloak. But I suspected Jake sounded like a thousand other veteran seamen who hung about the docks. No one seemed to know him.

"Are you hungry?" I asked Foley at last.

He grunted, looking worse than a drowned wharf rat. "When am I not?"

"Maybe if we stop to eat something, the rain will let up." I turned toward a tavern across the street.

"That's no kind of place for a female of good family," he said quickly. "Here, I have a thought."

He led me toward a respectable piece goods shop, two doors down the way, and stood me out of the rain, beneath the overhanging eaves. "It will take me but a minute to buy us hot tea and bread, maybe with some potted meat or cheese." As I counted out coins from my purse into his palm, he fixed me with a black glare. "Don't you even be thinkin' about movin' till I get back, Miss Dorsey."

I nodded automatically, no longer shocked that he, the servant, dared give orders to his mistress. I was too wet, tired, and hungry to care.

Foley turned to leave, then hesitated, touching the butt of the pistol tucked into his belt. Mama had given it to him to carry on the trip. I guessed he was contemplating leaving it with me, but he must have thought better of the idea. "All right, then. I'll be no more than a minute or two," he promised.

I watched him walk away, his shoulders bunched and shivering against the driving rain. As soon as he disappeared into the tavern, I looked up and down the street, feeling more closely watched than ever. I couldn't say why. People seemed more interested in getting out of the rain than worrying about me.

I waited anxiously. Minutes passed, and my feet grew stiff with cold. Where was Foley? I glared at the tavern door. A dozen more men had entered, but no one came out. Again, I let my eyes drift up and down the now-empty, rain-slick street.

In the shadowy mouth of an alley across the way, something moved. I narrowed my eyes, waited for someone to step out into the open. No one did.

A cat, I thought, or perhaps a mongrel dog scavenging for scraps. Again, something flashed forward, then darted back. A hand! It looked like a hand, gesturing toward me.

Slowly I crossed the slippery cobbles to the other side. I was several feet away from the alley when a voice whispered hoarsely, "Missy . . . over here."

"Yes?" I answered, chills dancing up my spine. Cautiously, I ventured into the narrow space between buildings, peered between rubbish heaps and wavering shadows of rags hanging from clotheslines. But I could see nothing, hear nothing more than the unrelenting splatter of the rain.

"Jake? Is that you?" I called out, my voice trembling. I stepped carefully around the splintered slats of broken crab pots, then climbed over a mound of tangled fish nets, slimy with seaweed.

Something scraped the wall behind me. I swung around with a shriek.

☆ CHARLIE ☆

JAKE MUST HAVE BEEN HIDING BEHIND THE RUBBISH pile, for his wide shoulders and enormous height suddenly rose up before me, blocking my way to the street.

"Now, girlie," his deep voice rumbled, "you'll let me finish sayin' me piece this time."

Even though this was the man I'd been searching for, the sight of him terrified me. Threatening words were my only protection and instinctively flew from my mouth. "My servant has a gun!"

"Does he, now. That smart Irish lad?" Jake chuckled,

rubbing his grizzly beard with the scarred knuckles of one hand. "And what would he be doin' with it if not killin' Brits?"

He was mocking me, the old rogue. Maybe the doctor was right and I'd walked into a trap. "Enough idle chatter," I stated, pretending the bravery of a stage heroine, although my heart was pounding and my legs felt as weak as a baby chick's. "Why have you been following me? What is it you want to tell me?"

Jake rolled his bleary eyes and said simply, "Why, to bring you word of yer brudder. I tole you that!"

I drew in a short, painful breath. "Charlie. Is he alive?"

"Alive . . . indeed, he is. And wantin' to see you, miss."

I dared not let myself believe him, not yet. The doctor might still be right about the man being a charlatan.

"Then it was *you* who sent the note by way of the peddler?" I ventured.

"Nay, nay." His drink-pinkened eyes twinkled with amusement. "That were your brudder's own doin'."

"Prove it," I demanded.

He chuckled. "Young Charles, he warned me you'd be a smart lass and not take my word or anyone else's for his fate."

"Take me to him," I ordered through trembling lips, wishing Foley would appear with his trusty pistol. Not that I'd want him to use it; I'd just feel safer in his company.

Jake shook his gray head and sighed. "Sech poor manners for a pretty miss. That's what I been tryin' to do for weeks, but you wouldn't let me."

I swallowed, still not willing to risk complete belief in anything he said until I saw Charlie in flesh and blood and heard an explanation from my brother's own lips.

"Come on then, lass. Follow me." He pushed past me and lumbered off toward the rear of the alley.

I hesitated. Foley had said he'd return momentarily, but he had already been gone nearly twenty minutes. I dared not miss this opportunity to be reunited with Charlie, if Jake spoke the truth. That in itself was a gamble, but what other choice did I have? I drew a deep breath and took off after the big man.

The alley ran into a maze of drenched, gray lanes that took us up a steep hill and away from the harbor. After close to a half mile of slogging through the rain past tenements and smelly refuse, the old man stopped at an abandoned shed. He opened the door and waved me inside.

"Charlie?" I called, promising God in a hundred ways that I'd be good, sweet-natured, and never complaining (very unlike my old self)—if only Jake wasn't lying to me.

Something rustled at the back of the shed, as if a small animal were digging itself out of a burrow. "Here," a clear, familiar voice stated.

I squinted into the darkness, my heart leaping in my breast with hope. Out from behind a pile of straw emerged a stooped figure, hobbling toward me with the aid of a crooked tree branch that had been whittled clean of bark and fashioned into a crutch. The figure's face was smeared with grime, and its hair hung raggedly around ears and jaw. Not Charlie . . . a mere street urchin. Or was it?

"At last I got through to you, Carrie."

I wouldn't have recognized my brother by sight, but for the teasing twinkle in his eyes as he straightened up and brushed limp strands of hair from his eyes.

"Charlie!" I cried. "Oh, Charlie, what has happened to you?"

He laughed and hugged me when I rushed at him. But he winced when I squeezed too hard. I quickly released him. "You've been terribly injured," I said. "Come, we must find you a physician."

"No," he said. "I'm healing, thanks to Jake. Besides, all the physicians are busy preparing to treat our soldiers and militias when the fighting begins."

"But what happened? We heard you were dead! I wouldn't believe it, but . . . why did Captain Moses say so if it wasn't true?"

A dull thud and grunt interrupted his answer. I spun toward the doorway of the shed in time to see my guide fall like an axed oak to the dirt floor. Standing over Jake was Foley, the butt of the pistol still raised over the spot where the man's head had been. It took Foley less than a second to flip the weapon and point its deadly muzzle at Charlie.

"No!" I shouted. "Foley, don't!"

Charlie pushed me out of the way and hobbled forward with effort. "Foley, it's me, Charles Dorsey. You remember me, don't you? From the stables . . . you saddled my horse for me often enough . . . the chestnut stallion, Duke."

Foley stood firm, his features rigid, but the gun that had been leveled at Charlie's heart slowly lowered toward the ground.

"The lad I knew as the young mistress's brother was a strappin' fella with the agility of a panther and a handsome face. Now explain yourself, knave, before I blast a hole through ya!"

I stepped closer to Charlie. "You'd better do as he says. He's a stubborn one and doesn't take orders very well at all."

"Fine," Charlie said, settling his weight onto the crutch for support. He glanced with concern at poor Jake on the ground. "I'll start with the night of my murder—the fifteenth of July," he began in a solemn tone. "That is when I first became aware someone wanted me dead . . . the moment I hit the cold water of the harbor."

"Then you didn't accidentally fall off the deck," I said, pleased I'd been right all along.

Charlie let out a dry laugh and shook his head. "Me?"

"Someone pushed you," I guessed.

"More likely threw me," he said.

As I listened to my brother begin his incredible tale, the sight of him became easier to take. His leg must have been shattered, and some internal injury made it difficult for him to stand straight for long or breathe without effort. But it was my dear Charlie, all right, underneath the dirt and pauper's rags. My heart glowed, and thankful tears trickled down my cheeks.

"I had taken watch that night," he explained. "The captain had announced that we would attempt to sail south for the bay and open sea under cover of darkness as soon as we had a moonless night. We were to run the blockade the first chance we got. The day had been spent in exhausting preparation for our escape from the British. By the time I was relieved of duty, I was unusually fatigued. So much so, I could barely hold my eyes open. I took immediately to my bunk, in the tiny cubby reserved for the cabin boy behind the captain's quarters. Soon I was fast asleep—so soundly, it seems, I didn't wake when someone bound my feet and hands with rope, then carried me onto the deck."

I let out a gasp of horror. Foley, I noticed, had allowed the pistol to rest at his side. His face was taut with concentration.

"I later thought about how it must have happened," Charlie continued. "I'm quite sure something potent was added to the cider one of the men brought me toward the end of my watch. Otherwise I would have been up from my bunk, swinging fists at anyone who tried to hog-tie me.

"But I was dead to the world with sleep. My first waking sensation was a sharp pain in my leg, then cold water rushing all around me. I must have hit the hull of the ship or a wooden pylon in falling, which broke my leg but also woke me from my drugged sleep. Lucky, in a way, because I immediately began to struggle."

"And you broke free of the ropes!" I shouted so loudly, Foley jumped in surprise.

"Not entirely," Charlie said. "I was able to slip out of the ropes at my wrists, but those around my ankles held fast. And the pain in my leg was nearly unbearable. Nevertheless I was able to reach the water's surface and hold my head above the spume. I couldn't swim very well, with only my arms free. I let the tide carry me away from the ship, thankful the water was warm, for I wouldn't have lasted ten minutes in the same water if it had been winter. The farther I drifted from her, the better, I believed—since it was someone onboard who had tried to drown me."

A low moan intruded on Charlie's story. He looked at Jake, lying beard-down in the dirt. We all watched the big man sit himself up unsteadily.

Jake groaned and rubbed his head. "Did a blazin' British shell come through here and take me down?"

"No," Charlie said, "the butt of what appears to be one of my father's dueling pistols. I'm sorry, Jake. My family hasn't treated you very well."

"Sorry," Foley mumbled guiltily.

"Jake is your friend," I said, having understood this much by now.

Charlie nodded. "He saved my life. Jake Tyler is an eastern shore waterman. He rakes in oysters from the shallow beds in the bay."

"And an occasional boy," Jake huffed, still looking a bit dazed by the blow to his noggin.

"Yes," Charlie said with a grateful smile. "He pulled me out of the water at dawn, near done in with exhaustion. Jake took me back to his house at Queenstown and, with his wife's help, set my leg, bandaged my bruised ribs, then put me to bed. I must have slept for a week before realizing where I was and what had happened."

"By then," I murmured, "we thought you were dead."

"Yes. I supposed you might, if anyone had reported me missing. But I didn't dare return to Elk Ridge for fear of bringing whatever danger had found me back to you and Mama. I needed to first find out who was responsible for tossing me to the fish, and why. So I paid a peddler to bring you and Mama a letter, assuring you both of my love and safety and that I would return soon. It also warned you of danger."

"And said I should trust only one person," I added.

"Yes, Jake here."

Jake rubbed his head and glared at me. "Small thanks do I get fer all my trouble."

"But the letter never reached us," I objected. "When the peddler arrived weeks later, he had lost the note to a British raiding party and could remember only snatches of the message."

Charlie nodded thoughtfully. "Jake was in Baltimore buying supplies for himself and his neighbors when he heard a girl questioning sailors about a boy who'd fallen overboard in the harbor. When you mentioned my name, he wondered if you were my sister, and he tried to talk to you."

"Oh no," I whispered. "I'm sorry, Jake. I was frightened and, you're right, terribly rude."

He dipped his head and smiled meekly. "S'pose I'm not the prettiest sight. And I'd treated meself to a coupla pints."

Charlie grinned at him fondly. "You always have a couple of pints in you." He turned back to me. "Jake came home, saying he had stopped a girl, thinking it was you. But he figured he'd gotten the wrong girl because she'd told him her brother was with her. And he knew from what I'd told him of our family that I was your only brother."

"True 'nough," Jake muttered.

"But he described you," Charlie continued. "I was sure it was you he'd seen. If you were asking around the city for me, I knew you hadn't received my letter."

"The peddler must have bided his time at every town along the way," I said.

Foley looked at me, as if to say: *Told you he wasn't to be trusted.*

I glanced apologetically at Jake. "Then you came all the way to Elk Ridge to try to speak to me again, but I thought you were a crazy man, out to do me harm."

"Sorry, lass," Jake muttered. "I get mighty thirsty when travelin'. Stopped at a tavern or two along the highway to wet my whistle."

"Ya musta visited every one of 'em between Baltimore and the plantation," Foley accused him. "How could ya expect a young lady of breedin' t' listen to ya in that state?"

Jake shrugged and gave me a bashful smile.

I drew a slow, long breath and made an effort to sort out all I'd learned. But Foley found words first. "The good of all this, thanks be t' the saints, is the Dorseys haven't lost a son and brother." Foley held the grip of the pistol out to Charlie. "Here, you'd best be takin' this, Master Charles."

"No," Charlie said, "you should keep it. I don't dare return to Elk Ridge yet."

"Because you still don't know who tried to kill you?" I asked.

"Yes," he said. "And if killing me is still important to someone, I would be putting both you and Mama in danger by my presence. First we must find the scoundrel behind what's happened and his reasons for choosing me as his target." He seemed about to say something else, but his gaze wavered, as if he was suddenly unsure whether or not he should go on.

"What, Charlie?" I begged. "If you know anything else that will help, please tell us."

He shook his head slowly. "It's nothing I can be certain of. There have been rumors on the docks. After I was off the *Liberty,* she made it through the blockade. Most people are saying it was amazing that not a single British ship challenged her."

Jake let out a sharp laugh. "Not so strange if the *Liberty* were in league with the British!"

I stared at him, shocked. "You mean, Captain Moses might be a spy for the enemy?"

"Not everyone in this country wants America to win the war," Charlie said in a grave voice. "It may be the entire crew knew of the deception, feared I might find out and give them away."

"How terrible," I breathed. But Jake's theory made a strange sort of sense. "If the crew were British spies and they were discovered, they'd be tried for treason and hanged if found guilty. Right?"

Foley nodded grimly. "That's enough reason for them t' have chucked Master Charles in the harbor."

"Yes," Charlie agreed. "But that might not be the

real or whole story. Until we find the entire truth, I must remain dead for all the world but the three of you." He fixed me with a solemn stare.

It suddenly struck me, what he was asking. "Do you mean, I can't tell anyone that you're alive? Not even Mama?"

"You mustn't yet. Her reaction would make the truth too obvious. No, as long as she and whoever is involved in this strange plot believe I'm dead, we have a chance of finding out who is responsible." He hobbled over to stand in front of Foley. "I entrust my mother's and sister's safety to you. Their lives are in your hands. What is your name?"

"Foley, sir. You know that."

"No, I mean your Christian name."

"Sean, sir. Sean Foley."

Charlie nodded. "Good, then. You keep that pistol close by you, Sean, whether you're here in Baltimore or back in the stables at Elk Ridge. You keep an eye out for trouble or strange happenings of any sort." He turned to me. "Be sure Sean knows where you and Mama are at all times, and don't leave Elk Ridge without him."

"Mama intends for us to move to Frederick tomorrow."

"Why?"

"The British," I said with a helpless shrug. "Dr. Macaphee says they have landed at Benedict and will surely attack either Washington or Baltimore within days. The plantation stands direct in their path if they march on Baltimore. He believes we must leave for our own safety."

Charlie frowned.

"What's wrong?" I asked.

After a moment, he let out a deep breath. "I hope he's wrong. If Elk Ridge isn't safe, I don't know where it will be. My guess is you should both remain there. Try to convince Mama and the doctor to stay, too. It's with the servants and in familiar surroundings you'll be best off. Foley?" He swung back to face the Irish stable boy. "Sean, that is, for we must count you as a friend, will you help us? Will you do what you can to protect my family?"

"I will," Sean Foley said, his chin set firm, his eyes as dark as the ocean's bottom. "On my mother's grave, I swear I will guard their lives, sir."

☆ THE PRESIDENT'S LETTER ☆

I WOULD HAVE TOLD CHARLIE I DIDN'T NEED SEAN Foley to protect me because I was fully capable of looking after myself. But having heard what had happened to my brother on the *Liberty* and how close he'd come to death, I decided I wouldn't mind having someone nearby I could trust.

Foley, that is Sean—for now, as queer as this may sound, I thought of him as a different person from the one who had driven me home from Philadelphia not so many weeks ago—talked no more on this trip than he had in the past. But I sensed this was a different sort of silence. A companionable warmth was shared by us. I believe it came about because we were bound by a secret—my brother was alive and had been the target of a murderous plot! Together, we were sworn to silence, and had vowed to help find Charlie's enemy.

When we arrived at Elk Ridge, Foley cooed the horse to a clomping stop, then jumped down from the driver's seat. He came around quickly to help me down from the carriage. "It will be difficult," he said, "keepin' your promise."

"You mean, not telling Mama?" I whispered, looking around to be sure no one was listening.

"Aye," he said. "Ya must be strong. You'll be achin' t' give her the grand news and comfort her after all her pain."

"I can manage," I said firmly.

"I . . . um—" He hesitated.

"Yes?" I prompted him.

He looked straight into my eyes and I didn't even mind, though he was still a servant. "If ya need anythin'. If anyone should accost ya or you're in danger—"

"I know where to find you. In the stables."

"Yes." He ducked his head, turned, and walked back to the carriage. By the time I had mounted the steps, he'd driven around the corner of the house toward the rear yards.

Mama's maid informed me that she was in her bedroom, resting before the evening meal. Dr. Macaphee appeared to be nowhere about. I slipped into the kitchen to ask Cook of his whereabouts.

She took her head out of the fireplace long enough to tell me the doctor had gone out for a ride, to see what news he could learn of the latest British position from passersby on the highway. Then she squinted at me and added, "You are the worst sight I ever did see, Miss Caroline, and you smells like a wet dog. Git yourself upstairs. I'll send Phoebe to help you clean up and change for dinner."

I took her word on my appearance, knowing full well how thoroughly my clothing and hair had been soaked by the rain. But the rain hadn't been the real cause of my odor. My shoes and the hems of my skirts and petticoats had sponged up filthy liquids, afloat with rank fish heads and human waste, that had puddled in the gutters and on the docks.

I do think Cook was being kind, for I've smelled many a hunting hound with a far more pleasant bouquet. I told her not to bother summoning Phoebe. I could take care of my own toilet.

In my bedroom, before pulling the heavy lace curtains over the window, I looked down into the yard. The carriage sat where Sean had stopped it. He stood beside the horse, unhitching it from the rails. Just as I was about to let the curtain drop, he shot a quick look directly up at my window. I lifted my hand in a wave, but he immediately returned his attention to the horse, as if he feared being seen looking at me.

With a sigh, I dropped the curtain. Sean was right: We had to be wary, guard our hearts and our secrets. Any sudden change in attitude between us, as mistress and servant, would arouse suspicion.

But whose suspicion? For some reason, I immediately thought of the woman I'd glimpsed wandering the woods' edge. Could she be somehow connected with this foul business? Then there was the actual attack on Charlie. Had it been related to the war, as Charlie and his friend Jake believed? Or might his near-murder be the evil work of another sort of enemy—someone we hadn't yet suspected?

I spent the next hour trying to compose a list of people who might wish to harm Charlie or heap more tragedy on the Dorseys. I struggled with the chore. How could Charlie possibly have any enemies, when he was so sweet natured and generous of spirit? But my father, though an equally good person, did have enemies. He had supported President Madison against determined political foes, who would still seize power if they could. I might ask Dr. Macaphee to name individuals who had spoken against my father, anyone who might have hated him enough to want to hurt his family, even after his death.

A voice from the hallway startled me out of my dark thoughts. I lifted my head to listen and heard Mama direct one of the maids to ready her jewelry box for travel. A moment later there came a knock on my door.

"Caroline? May I come in?"

"Yes, Mama," I said, slipping the sheet of paper on which I'd been writing into one of the tiny cubby-holes in my escritoire. Turning away from the desk, I smiled at her. "I was just writing a letter."

"Good, that's good," she murmured distractedly as her eyes swept the room. "Amelia will be glad to hear you're safe, although I'm sure she'll be sad you're not returning immediately to school."

I suppose she assumed I had no one but Amelia to whom I might write. "Yes," I murmured.

She glanced down at her hands, and it was only then I noticed the brownish envelope, sealed in red wax, that rested in her fingertips.

"Is that for me?" I asked. If Captain Moses had seen fit to answer my query, it would be interesting to see what he had to say—even though I now expected it would be lies.

"Yes," Mama said, frowning. "I didn't even look at the name on the front and started to open it. I don't see why Cousin James would be writing to—"

"Oh!" I cried without thinking, "the president! He promised he would write if he discovered anything about Charlie." I eagerly snatched the letter from her hand.

Mama looked surprised. "So now you've even enlisted Mr. Madison in your search? What does our busy president have to say to a young girl in the middle of a war?" Clearly she didn't take this correspondence seriously.

I looked down at the letter in my hand, wishing Mama would go away to let me read Mr. Madison's message in private. I still had to protect Charlie's secret. But she seemed far too curious. I expected she wouldn't leave me until she was satisfied as to the letter's contents.

"I will read it aloud to you," I said, my heart fluttering anxiously in my chest. At least then I might be able to omit parts I couldn't risk her hearing. "It looks rather long. Maybe we should sit in the parlor."

She smiled. "Yes. Yes, let's do that. We may not have another chance to enjoy my lovely room."

We settled ourselves on opposite ends of the chaise longue nearest the windows, for the best light. Then I began to read:

"'My dear friend, Caroline Dorsey:

"'As promised, I have inquired among my officers, cabinet, and friends with regard to your brother, Charles, who was reported to have drowned on the night of July fifteenth in Baltimore Harbor. Although I have been unable to ascertain any facts relevant to his fate, I do herein report to you several issues of distressing nature. These issues may, I fear, already have had severe consequences for your family—'"

Mama drew a sharp breath, interrupting me. "Oh dear, maybe I should read this myself." She reached for the letter.

"No," I said, drawing it away from her, "let me continue. Mr. Madison's script is difficult to make out, and my eyes are better than yours." My fingers felt glued to the paper with their own perspiration. My mouth had gone utterly dry. Apparently the president hadn't discovered, as I had, that Charlie was most definitely alive. But I wanted to be sure he didn't let drop a clue too obvious for Mama or anyone else to guess the truth. I took a deep breath and plunged on. . . .

"'I've supplied the details of your brother's case to several of my naval officers familiar with ships that call Baltimore their home port. Many of these vessels are, as you know, privateers loyal to America. However, two officers have informed me that the captain of the *Liberty* is under grave suspicion of espionage for the king. It is my conjecture that your beloved brother may have discovered Captain Moses's true loyalties and intended to reveal the *Liberty*'s treachery. If so, it seems likely he may have been silenced by the king's spies.'"

Mama was shaking her head as tears trickled from her eyes. She cupped her hands around her mouth as if to contain a scream of protest.

I stopped reading and laid a hand on her trembling shoulder. "Mr. Madison offers no proof. There's nothing to say that Charlie is dead. We must hold out hope."

"I fear it is as you've said from the start," she sobbed. "He didn't fall of his own clumsiness. I should have known . . . poor Charles . . . I should have listened to you, Caroline."

She looked so very sad. I cursed my promise to Charlie. It wasn't fair of him to expect me to deceive Mama so cruelly! Yet I understood why he believed temporarily lying to her was for her own and my safety. And for Charlie's protection, too. If silencing him had been so very important before, these dangerous men wouldn't hesitate to try again if they discovered he still lived.

"Mama," I said gently, "there *is* hope. If I was right before, about Charlie not drowning by accident, you must believe me now. There is hope for all of us."

"How?" she asked weakly.

"I-I can't explain."

"Do you mean these demons may have only hid him away somewhere, not killed him?"

"Perhaps," I answered lamely.

She sighed and wiped at her damp eyes with the sleeve of her gown. "I fear they may be too ruthless to take that chance. They would worry he might escape." She sighed heavily, then lifted her chin and stood up. "But, if you like, you can pray this is so, for both of us. Now I must finish preparations for our leaving."

I glanced down at the letter in my lap. There was more written, which she hadn't pressed me to recite or didn't realize was there. I folded the page on itself to conceal the unread portion. "No, we should stay here."

"But Caroline, it's dangerous. You've heard what Dr. Macaphee has said. The enemy's troops may well choose to move along the toll road to reach Baltimore."

I thought quickly. "But if Charlie, by some miracle, is still alive—how will he find us if we're not here?"

She hesitated, and I could see a shadow of doubt flicker across her face. "It's not likely, child," she said sadly.

"But it might be. Then we would not be here if he needs our help."

Mama stared at me, then shrugged wearily. "I suppose it won't hurt to wait awhile longer."

She left me in the parlor and, only when I was certain she wasn't returning to put in a final word, did I dare open the letter again and finish silently reading Mr. Madison's words:

You should be aware, dear Caroline, although Captain Moses and his crew of British sympathizers have no doubt sailed far away from Baltimore by now, his coconspirators are probably still in our midst. Spies in our cities and countryside will have informed Moses of our army's and militias' locations, the numbers of men in each unit, and our sad lack of weapons. They will have scouted out possible locations for landing British soldiers. And all of this information has by now, I suspect, been given to Captain Moses, then delivered by him to the British General Ross.

A chill raced through my body and my chest tightened, preventing me from breathing. No wonder the captain had to get rid of Charlie! He couldn't let him witness his meeting with the British. But why had he agreed to take Charlie on as a cabin boy in the first place? The man wouldn't want outsiders around to witness his traitorous actions. He must have known Charlie wouldn't turn against America.

Unless, I thought as I gulped down air, conjuring up an even more terrible possibility . . . unless someone had intended all along for Moses to kill Charlie!

I closed my eyes and shivered. Who had recommended Moses and the *Liberty* to us? Macaphee! Was it possible we had so gravely misjudged the gentleman from Virginia?

I crumpled the letter in my shaking hands. Charlie wouldn't have been a danger to the British cause in the war, until Macaphee put him in the middle of the espionage plot. Why had the doctor done it? What bitter resentment had the doctor held against Charlie or my family?

Stuffing the letter inside my dress sleeve, I ran from the parlor, out the front door of the house, down the steps, and around the back toward the stables. Sean was mucking out one of the horse's stalls and looked up when he heard my running steps.

His face suddenly darkened. He stood straight and propped the shovel against the wooden rails. Looking around to be certain no one was within hearing, he asked, "What's happened?"

I was out of breath and found it impossible to speak in anything but anguished gasps. "A letter . . .

from Mr. Madison . . ." I swallowed, drew a deep breath, and tried again. I delivered a brief summary of the letter's shocking contents and my theory about Macaphee. "And all of this means that the doctor, while on his so-called business trips, might have been spying on our army and gathering information for the British to help them defeat us!"

Sean let out a low whistle. "This would explain a great deal, miss."

"Yes," I agreed, "if it's true. I mean about the doctor. President Madison's letter spoke only of Captain Moses, the *Liberty*, and unnamed spies."

Scowling, Sean scratched his head, pulled a small bug from among the black hairs, and flicked it casually with his fingernail across the stall. "There is one part of this I don't yet understand. If the doctor is a spy, why would he arrange for your brother t' sail on the *Liberty*? Why not put the boy on another ship instead of riskin' his discoverin' their secret?"

"That's exactly what I've been wondering," I said flatly. "To put Charlie on the *Liberty* intentionally meant Captain Moses would have no choice but to kill Charlie, sooner or later." I held my head in my hands and squeezed my eyes shut, trying to think of reasons why the man who had pretended to be our friend had turned against us.

Sean paced the stall, automatically stepping around piles of horse droppings. At last, he stopped and looked down at me. "Money," he said.

"What money?"

"Your family's."

I stared at him as I tried to grasp his reasoning. "But the doctor has plenty of money. He has estates in Virginia, beautiful houses, and many investments. He was always riding off to check on his accounts or withdraw money he feared the British would take from him and—"

Sean was shaking his head at me. "Nay, miss. He was doin' their dirty business as you've said. And if he were a spy, he wouldn't be fearin' America's enemies. Whatever he now owns, they'd let him keep, and they probably promised him more after they won the war, in payment for his services to 'em."

"Then he might be as poor as a . . . as a stable

boy!" I groaned, too late realizing my words might sound unkind.

He nodded, not looking particularly offended. "Right. And I'd be guessin' that he's had his eye on your family's wealth for a long time."

I let his words sink in. "He asked Mama to marry him," I murmured. "She told him no."

Sean shrugged. "Marriage would have gotten him what he wanted, regardless of the outcome of the war. If the Americans win, and your brother—bein' the only boy in the family—was dead, Macaphee eventually would have the entire Dorsey fortune to himself. And if England wins, he might be given the land by the king, anyway." Foley suddenly looked even more worried. "Do you still have the president's letter?"

"Yes, here." I pulled it from my sleeve.

He reached for the rumpled paper, but I held on to it. "That's evidence against the captain," I said. "I should keep it in a safe place."

Sean looked around the stable. "It will be safer here with me. If Macaphee suspects you have proof against him, he will look in the house first."

I tensed at his refusal to follow my wishes, but I could see the determination in his vivid blue eyes. He met my stare with defiance, and I knew there was little use arguing with the stubborn boy. Besides, I thought, he may be right. I handed over the letter.

"But how shall I convince Mama that Macaphee is a traitor? She thinks of him as a trusted friend."

"Ya must tell her nothin' yet. If she knows about the doctor, she may give all away by her reaction to him. It's not yet time to act."

I wrapped my arms around my body, as if to physically hold in the secrets piling up inside. "Yes, but I don't know how much longer I can keep all of this silent!"

"You are strong, Caroline Dorsey," he said, gripping my arm for a moment. "You are strong and ya will do what you must t' protect your family."

I smiled at him gratefully. "Nonetheless, I will be glad to know you still have that pistol on you."

He patted a lumpy spot beneath his loose homespun shirt. "If you call, I will come. I'll not be lettin' ya down, miss."

☆ SEAN'S SACRIFICE ☆

AS I CROSSED THE YARD, I PASSED MR. BLACK. HE shot me a sharp, questioning look, but I owed him no explanations. I gave him a haughty toss of my head, letting him know my business was my own, and marched on toward the house. He would probably ask Sean why I had been so long in the stables with him. I would let Sean make whatever excuse he liked to keep himself out of trouble. He would be much the better off without having to match my story.

I walked into the foyer, which was now bare of portraits. It looked sadly empty and echoed with my footsteps. Ready to depart in a rush, Mama had packed all the paintings away and placed them in one room with our silver, linens, and other valuables. I hoped my argument for waiting, in case Charlie showed up, would hold her until we could reveal the whole truth.

I started up the staircase to my room, but felt a hand fall on my arm. With a shocked whimper I turned to face Dr. Macaphee himself.

"Where have you been, Caroline?" he asked. The heavy line of his russet brows lowered ominously over his eyes.

I couldn't make my mouth work for several seconds. "To the stables," I managed at last, fearing he might have seen me and would be suspicious if I lied. "I wanted to check on the horses. I feared the grooms might not have them ready, should we need to leave with little warning."

He observed me from the long slope of his nose. "Yet, only a short while ago, you convinced your mother not to leave Elk Ridge at all. That seems contradictory behavior, don't you agree?"

His voice had a hard, dangerous edge, and his eyes were dark and predatory like those of a hawk. I felt small and hunted, suddenly helpless.

Words tumbled out of my mouth. "I-I don't believe we should leave our home unless it is absolutely necessary. But being prepared is always a good thing, is it not?" I glanced hastily around the foyer, listening for sounds from other rooms. "Where is my mother?"

"Above, in her room, changing into traveling clothes," he said briskly. "Just as you should be. Go up and finish packing now, Caroline."

"No." I bolted for the stairs, but Macaphee was faster.

His hand whipped out and latched around my arm, pulling me back off the first step. His fingers squeezed so hard, my hand went numb.

"Stop!" I cried. "You're hurting me! Mama!" I shouted up at the second-floor landing as I struggled.

My mother appeared at the top of the stairs. She looked down over the carved wooden banister at us. The anger she'd obviously intended to direct at me for my noisy misbehavior quickly shifted its focus when she saw the doctor holding me forcibly. "Lawrence, what are you doing to that child?"

"She's hysterical, refusing to leave when there is nothing else left to do."

"Release her!" Mama ordered, glaring down at him.

His fingers eased slightly, then dropped away. I hastily dashed out of his reach, rubbing the throbbing sensation away.

"We should stay here!" I cried, running breathlessly up the stairs. "This is our home. Besides, the roads are too dangerous to travel now. British soldiers are everywhere!"

I was counting on the servants hearing me. Should the doctor attempt to force us to leave, or try to harm us while we were at Elk Ridge, they would protect us. But if we left the plantation, we would be alone with a dangerous spy on the open road. Anything could happen there. Perhaps another accident, like the one he'd planned for Charlie, only on dry land.

"Caroline," Mama said, slowly descending to meet me halfway down the stairs, "Lawrence didn't mean any harm, I'm sure. He's just upset and concerned for us. I've reconsidered. We must leave."

I couldn't believe her sudden change of mind. "But, Charlie . . . we—"

"No," she interrupted me with surprising firmness when we reached the first landing together, "listen to what the doctor has to say. The news is grim and allows us no alternative."

I looked reluctantly down at Macaphee, still standing in the foyer, staring up at us but now with a satisfied expression. As if he'd won after all.

"Yesterday, the British army met American forces at Bladensburg in a brief battle," he stated, the words sending an icy chill up my spine. "The Americans were no match for them."

I looked at Mama, and she nodded. "It's sadly true. A few minutes ago two farmers headed for Baltimore stopped in to warn us. They were at Bladensburg among those who escaped a terrible slaughter. Those of our army and militia who weren't killed or wounded took to the hills to save themselves." All this she had learned while I was out at the stables.

"Mr. Madison, is he all right?" I cried.

"He wasn't there," Macaphee said. "At least no one saw him on the battlefield. I expect he's on the run like the rest of his army."

I gaped at Macaphee, amazed at the half smile tugging at his thick lips. He seemed no longer concerned with hiding his delight in America's hardship. But Mama appeared unaware of his elated mood.

"Then, early today," she continued mournfully, walking me the rest of the way down the stairs, "the British army took Washington City with little resistance. They burned to the ground every public building but the patent office."

"The entire city!" I cried in dismay. "Even Congress? Even the president's house?"

"Yes." Mama sighed and looked at the doctor, who arranged his expression into a sober mask. "Lawrence fears Baltimore will be next, unless Congress has already had time to meet and surrender to the British."

And that would mark the end of our country—the end of the United States of America.

"As I've said from the start," Macaphee proclaimed,

unable to keep his lips from lifting into a nervous grin, "there is no hope."

Mama glanced at him disapprovingly. "I fail to understand why you choose this dark moment, Doctor, to gloat over your talent for prophesy." I could hear the irritation in her voice, even if he didn't know her well enough to realize what a serious mistake he'd made. She turned away from him to me. "Come, Caroline. We'll take the largest carriage and only carry away what will fit in it with us."

"No," I said, "I'm staying." She wouldn't leave without me, I was sure.

Her eyes flamed, and she stepped toward me. "There is no time for argument, child! Fetch whatever you need to travel, then join me and the doctor in the carriage."

"No," I said, "not with *him.*" I looked pointedly at Macaphee.

"Why on earth not?" she demanded, at the end of her patience.

I hesitated, but could see no other way out.

"Lawrence Macaphee is a traitor. He has been helping the British all along. He is a spy!"

I felt the heat of the doctor's eyes on me, but refused to look at him.

Mama fell back a step, staring at me in horror, as if she'd just observed horns sprouting from my head. "Stop it, Caroline!"

I moved toward her even as the doctor also edged forward, a tense smile flickering over his lips.

"It's true," I insisted. "You heard what Mr. Madison said in his letter—Captain Moses is a British sympathizer, in league with other men who want England to win the war. One of those men is Dr. Macaphee. The doctor put Charlie on the *Liberty* because he *wanted* him killed. In case the British lost, he could still marry you and take Papa's and Grandpapa's estates, because there would be no boy in the family to inherit them."

Mama shook her head in disbelief. "But Lawrence is a wealthy man. He has property of his own. He has no need for such deceit." She lifted her eyes to the doctor for his reassurance.

He shrugged. "The girl's claims are ridiculous!" He let go an arrogant snort. "The British are winning the war. In a matter of days, there probably will be a formal surrender and Elk Ridge will fall into their hands along with the rest of the country. But it's certainly none of my doing, ladies."

He reached for Mama's hand and, I think, would have kissed it, but she stepped quickly back from him, her eyes suddenly wary, her manner suspicious. "Maybe my daughter is right about one thing; we should stay here for the time being."

"Margaret, be sensible. The British will mow down all before them in the heat of their victory after burning Washington. I cannot stay here to protect you and your property against an entire army. You and your daughter must come with me, for your own safety."

"No," she said, in a low voice as strong as any my father had ever used. "We will go our own way or stay here to face the British. If my daughter believes so fervently that this is best, I will trust her instincts, for I suspect mine have been clouded of late."

I moved close to her and watched Macaphee's reaction, suddenly afraid. He looked confused for only a minute, then lunged unexpectedly toward us, grasping Mama's wrist in one hand and mine in his other. "If you won't come gently, you foolish women," he growled, "you shall come because I make you do so!"

He dragged us toward the door as Mama stared at him in shock.

I set up a horrid shrieking and wailing, calling out to everyone in the house and the stables. But mostly it was Sean's name I screeched as loudly as I was able.

Macaphee paid no heed. He hauled us onto the veranda and down the steps to the gravel drive, where a carriage waited with Mr. Black standing at the horses' heads.

"Mr. Black, stop him! Stop this traitor from taking us!" Mama cried.

Mr. Black's always-angry-looking face twisted in confusion. "Say there, sir!" he shouted. "Unhand the ladies. What is this? What is this?"

"Keep your distance, man!" the doctor warned. "Do you want your mistress raped by British soldiers?

I'm taking the women to safe ground, for their own good."

"No!" I protested. "Don't let him leave with us! He's a British spy! Please, someone stop him!"

Mr. Black didn't lose a second. He rushed at Macaphee, but the evil man quickly shifted his grip to my throat. "Come closer and I will snap the girl's neck."

The stable master froze mid-stride and stared helplessly at Mama.

By now, half the household staff, including Cook and most of the gardeners and stable boys, had appeared in the yard and gathered around the carriage, looking on with worried expressions.

"Stand back, I say!" the doctor bellowed. "If you've any sense, people, you'll be thinking of your own hides. Do you suppose the British army will be kind to servants of Madison's cousins?"

I sensed a shifting within the circle, then one figure stepped from among them. Sean Foley was holding the pistol Charlie had given him. He aimed it at Macaphee. "You'll be lettin' the ladies go now, sir," he said in an unnaturally polite voice. "Or I fear I'll hafta blow your schemin' head clear off your ugly body."

I felt Macaphee's fingers quiver at my throat, as if about to squeeze, then slowly release. I grabbed Mama's hand and pulled her away, leaving the doctor to face Sean's pistol.

I yearned to shout, "Shoot him! Shoot him, Sean!" For the man had deceived us all and tried to kill Charlie, and it wasn't his fault he hadn't succeeded. But I kept my wishes to myself so as not to distract Sean.

"What do you think you are doing, boy?" the doctor sneered.

"I'm invitin' ya t' leave the Dorsey land, without delay," Sean said, gesturing toward the road with the pistol. "We'll not be wantin' t' see ya around here again."

"I'm not leaving without Margaret and her daughter," the doctor stated. "They need my protection; the British will listen to me. Ross has promised to give me whatever I want." He turned to Mama, no longer pretending innocence, a wildly excited glaze over his eyes. "I can ask for Elk Ridge as my prize for aiding the Crown. No one else shall have it. You and Caroline will live with me, as my wife and daughter. I have it all planned, don't you see? Come now, enough of this nonsense."

Mama's eyes burned, but her words were as cold as a January morning. "I would give up all I own before marrying a man who sold his own country."

"Go!" I told Macaphee.

Before the word had completely left my lips, the doctor swung around with a fierce look in his eyes and dived for Sean's pistol. It happened so fast, I barely caught a blur of dark-colored frock coat and the shocked look on Sean's face. They both had their hands on the weapon and fell in a heap on the ground, struggling for possession of it.

"Do something!" I screamed at Mr. Black.

He launched himself at the two struggling figures, but the heel of Macaphee's boot caught him hard on the chin, and the stable master went down, unconscious.

I leaped forward. Mama threw her arms around me and held me back with surprising strength. "No, Caroline! You could be killed!"

The single crack of the gun made me cry out and

wince with fear. I shut my eyes, unable to look. The crowd was silent, watching . . . waiting. Slowly, I forced my eyes open.

Sean and Macaphee had frozen in combat, sprawled in thc dust, their arms and legs tangled. They looked expectantly at each other as if about to ask a question. Then the stable boy's face drained of color, and he let out a pained gasp.

"No!" I screamed. "No, not Sean!"

Mama held me tight. I watched in horror as Sean slumped on the ground. His face rolled into the dirt.

Dr. Macaphee pushed himself up off of the Irish boy and pried the pistol from his slack fingers while tearing the small leather ammunition pouch from Sean's belt. In a flash he had reloaded shot and powder. He held the gun before him as a warning, brushed the dust from his clothing, and dragged in gulps of air to restore his breathing.

"Now," he said, his voice rattling in his throat, "all of you will stand back and allow me to take the Dorsey ladies to Baltimore to welcome General Ross." Swinging the weapon in a slow arc, he eyed every one of our household, letting them know he would use the gun again should anyone try to stop him. Then he aimed the pistol's muzzle at the side of my head. "Margaret, you will board the carriage without further objection, or you will lose your last child before your very eyes."

"Mama, we can't—"

"Hush, Caroline!" she choked out, her eyes wide with fear. "Climb into the carriage." She pushed me toward it.

The doctor cautiously followed us. He mounted the driver's seat, slapped the reins on the horses' rumps, and away we rumbled, his captives.

I turned to look behind us as our carriage sped away. Our dear, loyal Sean lay in a dark red pool, unmoving. Cook threw herself down on him, wailing, while others tried to raise a stunned Mr. Black to his feet. If they could have helped us, I knew they would have.

I felt Mama's hands pull me to her, and I wept against her breast for Sean Foley as bitterly as I'd ever wept for Charlie when I'd feared him dead.

☆ THE BATTLE OF BALTIMORE ☆

MAMA AND I HELD EACH OTHER AS THE DOCTOR hawed the horses on toward Baltimore. The carriage traveled at a reckless speed, bumping and banging over the road, veering dangerously around slower wagons, coaches, and people on foot. Macaphee kept the pistol close to his side on the driver's seat, giving us no chance of escape without grave risk.

As he drove on at a breakneck pace, he jabbered unceasingly about the British general, whom he spoke of as a great hero.

"Ross, he's a man who knows how to play out a

war and win!" he shouted above the thunder of the horses' hooves. "I've word he hardly missed a meal after routing that cowardly mob of Americans at Bladensburg. Marched his troops straight on to Washington City the very next morning. Breakfasted on the meal the first lady left for Madison before she fled the president's house with her few pathetic treasures." He laughed loudly, throwing back his head of wild red hair, gloating over the victory he could see coming. "Ah, we'll be treated like royalty in Baltimore once Ross arrives!" he cackled.

"Oh, do shut up, Lawrence!" Mama shouted at him.

He pretended not to hear her. For miles he continued congratulating himself and his English friends on their upcoming victory and delighted in America's great shame at allowing her capital city to be reduced to ashes.

I shut out his boasting and closed my eyes, trying not to envision Dolley's beautiful home as a charred ruin, desperately wanting to forget another memory that was even more horrid: Sean, who had so gallantly defended us, stretched out in the dirt in his own blood.

My stomach clenched in a painful knot, and I quaked from head to foot with sorrow at his brave sacrifice and fear that Mama and I might end up the same. But with the passing miles, terror turned to a slow-boiling rage. Whether or not the British had beaten us, I could *not* allow Macaphee to destroy my family. And I wouldn't let Sean's death at this evil man's hands go unavenged! I vowed in my heart to see him punished.

As we neared Baltimore the toll road narrowed and became clogged with men, women, and children—brown-skinned and white, clothed in all variety of garments from costly, tailored suiting to rags. They marched in groups toward the city. Some of the men carried long guns and leather ammunition pouches; others wielded only clubs or had strapped knives in cloth sheaths to their waists. Market wagons loaded with supplies wove between them, stirring up dust, wearing new ruts in the road. The steady parade of people leaving the city days before was nothing to this rush into it.

"Fools," Macaphee muttered, snapping the reins to make the horses gallop faster. "They're marching to their own deaths, don't they know? Ross will have no pity for those who try to defend the city against the king's army."

I could stand no more of his inane boasting. Lurching forward, I grabbed him from behind by his collar and would have choked him to his last breath had not Mama pulled me off him when his right hand reached for the pistol.

"Madam, if you cannot control your daughter"—he coughed, his eyes red and streaming as he waved the weapon over his shoulder at us—"I will dispose of her and be glad of it."

"Caroline! Please God, don't anger him more. I can't lose you, too!" She dragged me back onto the leather seat beside her and held me fast. I had thought her still weak from the long-reaching effects of the fever, but her strength was remarkable at this moment.

I, by contrast, felt as frail and powerless as a newborn kitten. Perhaps that was why I then broke my promise to Charlie.

His motive for hiding the truth of his survival had been, largely, to protect Mama and me from danger. The way I looked at our current situation, we were neck deep in it already. Any sort of comfort I could give my mother now would be a blessing to her.

Besides, I could not say what might happen to us in Baltimore. There was a fair chance both Mama and I would die within this or the next day—if not by Macaphee's hand, then in the battle between the Americans and British. Perish, she still believing her son had gone before her. Me, with a lie weighing down my soul.

I looked up at her strained face and pulled myself erect on the seat, moving my lips close to her ear. "Don't say anything, just listen," I whispered.

Her body tightened, but not a sound escaped her.

"I've seen Charlie. Macaphee plotted with Captain Moses to drown him for our fortune, but his plan failed." From the rapid flutter of her eyelashes, I knew she was listening hard to my words. Whether or not she believed them, I couldn't say. "Charlie was rescued by an old waterman. He's alive, Mama."

Her body trembled. She blinked, staring steadily ahead without giving any other indication she understood me.

"I swear, on brave Sean Foley's soul—God give him rest—Charlie is alive and hiding in Baltimore. He only stayed away, hoping to spare us danger." I grabbed her stiff hands in mine and squeezed them tightly. "You shall see him again for yourself, and we *will* survive. I promise."

I don't know where I found those words to encourage her and can't, to this day, say whether or not I believed them myself. Perhaps they were no more than a prayer recited aloud, as soldiers murmur to themselves before battle, to make themselves brave. But I must have sounded convincing enough, because she looked at me with wide, tear-filled eyes that were suddenly alive with hope.

As we neared the city limits, the long blocks of row houses, two-storied shops, and merchants' warehouses, all of red brick, came into view. Macaphee slowed the team to a trot. The horses' breaths rattled and wheezed in their chests, for he'd kept them at a gallop for many miles without rest.

The doctor eyed the vast ramparts of rubble and earth that had been thrown up by Baltimore's citizens to defend their city. Towering piles topped with sharpened wooden stakes were manned by hundreds of men and women carrying firearms and clubs, iron rakes, and long-tined pitchforks. In an occasional break in the fortifications crouched an ominous black iron cannon. Its balls of shot, bigger than a man's fist, stood ready in neat pyramids. Macaphee frowned, looking vaguely worried. "Where have all these people come from?" he muttered.

A man walking beside us glanced up solemnly. "From all around the countryside, brother. The militias from Bladensburg have regrouped too. This be our last stand."

"No king's army will take Bawl'imer!" cried a man who overheard us.

"Baltimore will stand—or we'll die with her!" shouted a woman in rough men's clothing, a young child with dirty cheeks clutching her pant leg.

"Preposterous," Macaphee grumbled under his

breath. He turned around on the driver's seat to face Mama. "They can't actually believe they have a chance of holding off a professional army with a few cannonballs and sticks!"

"Lawrence," she said, "I believe they won't turn and run this time. Your English friends will face a true battle."

As there were plenty of people about, I considered calling out for help. But I knew Macaphee held his firearm at ready. If someone tried to help us escape, the doctor would be just as quick to use his pistol again. I did not wish anyone else to die for our sake.

This made me think of Sean again, and tears instantly burned my eyes.

Mama's arm came around my shoulders, as if she knew. "Courage, my girl," she whispered in my ear. "We must wait our chance."

The carriage came to a stop in front of a house on Boston Street in Fell's Point, not far from the waterfront. Most of the neighborhood shops had been boarded up, and more barricades had been built across the streets, but I wondered how much these piles of rubbish might really help. If the British make it this far, I thought sadly, we've lost the war and our country.

I prayed the outer walls and our brave defenders would hold them.

"Out of the carriage!" Macaphee ordered. "This is where we will stay for the time being."

Holding his pistol in clear view, apparently not worried that anyone might see it, as everyone in the street seemed to be carrying weapons, he waved us toward the door of a narrow row house. Without knocking, he opened it and pushed us into the dim interior. It took a moment for my eyes to adjust to the lack of light, but I could soon define the small dimensions of the room.

The ceiling was so low, I was surprised when Macaphee ducked through the doorway, then stood straight in the middle of the room. The place stank of mold and spoiled food and damp rock, for the walls were unplastered and dripped greenish moisture.

A woman stood beside a table, observing Macaphee as if she had expected him.

"Light a lamp, for God's sake!" he barked at her. "Can't you see we have guests?"

She winced at his rough command, and at first I thought she must be a servant. But then I noticed the low, sloping brows that met in the middle of her forehead, and the cold gray eyes so much like the doctor's. Her hair, though covered by a dingy cotton cap, poked out in rust-colored snarls around her face. When she turned her head, something about her profile looked familiar. I was certain I'd seen her before, though I couldn't at first recall where.

"This is my sister, Emma," Macaphee said as he bustled about the room, peering into crude pottery canisters on the shelf above the fireplace. "Have you no tea, woman? No food to offer our guests?" he demanded, scowling at her.

She gave a crude laugh. "Not without money, I don't, and maybe not even then. You've seen all them soldiers and farmers out there. They've bought up every scrap, leaving not so much as a crust for a simple woman like me." She glared at my mother. "*Her* and her fancy house with her servants waitin' on her . . . I'll bet she's got plenty in her larder. Why didn't you bring a nice ham and some new potatoes with you, Larry?"

Macaphee wheeled on her, his fist raised. "Insolence!" he roared. For a moment I thought he would strike her a terrible blow. But she ducked out of his way as if she'd had long practice in avoiding his temper.

"Go find some food," he said, tossing a handful of coins at her. "You can't expect your new sister-in-law to go hungry in this ill-kept house of yours!"

Emma scooped up the coins and, casting him a sulky look, disappeared through the low doorway.

By nightfall of the next day I thought I would go mad from being cooped up in the smelly hovel. It wouldn't have been so bad a place to live, I thought, if Emma had bothered to keep it clean. But she tossed food scraps into the corners and let them congeal into lumps of gray filth or else they were eaten by the rats I could hear scurrying around in the dark at night.

The chamber pots, though emptied each morning into the gutter outside the door, weren't scrubbed out afterward. They brought the revolting scent of urine back into the shabby room, which seemed to be all there was of her home. A back room had been walled off, as was the upstairs, presumably to provide small apartments for other tenants. We could hear them shuffling about, now and then—larger versions of our furry roommates.

We slept on a straw mat on the floor and ate two at a time, taking turns sitting in the pair of broken chairs at the wobbly table. We listened to frantic voices of people rushing through the streets, to wagons creaking and groaning with loads of rubble to add to the battlements. Through the single window I could see a small section of the harbor. Directly across the narrow, gray-green wedge of water stood Fort McHenry. The American flag that always flew over the fort was being lowered.

"Smart lads." Macaphee chortled gleefully. "They're giving it up!"

I looked at Mama, and she had tears in her eyes. After all the preparations, weren't we Americans even going to put up a fight? Would our country give up so easily? I hoped Charlie wasn't watching. I knew how bitterly disappointed he'd be.

Then a flash of color caught my eye, and I looked back at the fort. My heart stopped for a moment, then leaped joyfully in my chest, and I cried out. "No! Oh, look! Look, Mama!"

I pulled her over to the window and pointed. There, flapping in the salty breeze, a massive banner ten times or more the size of the other—its colors vibrant even from this distance—rose slowly up the tall pole at the summit of the gray stone fort. She was the most enormous flag I'd ever seen, and I judged from the cheer that went up all around the harbor that she was a welcome sight to our defenders, too.

Each of the fifteen white stars on a field of brilliant blue must have been as big as a meat platter. One of the fifteen alternating red and white stripes might have been as wide as the window through which we now stared in amazement. I imagined I could hear the crack of her canvas as she snapped in the wind—or maybe I really did hear it. It was a wonderful, brave sound.

"Arrogance!" Macaphee shouted. "A last, foolish act of defiance—that's what *that* is!" He pushed us away from the window and slammed the shutters closed, casting the room into darkness. I could hear him fumbling for a candle. "We'll see how long that rag flies. Ross's men will shred it on their bayonets before the day is out!"

Mama and I found each other with our eyes as the candle he lit gave out a weak orange glow. I smiled at her, and she smiled back. Our soldiers in the fort had not yet given up. This seemed a sign that all was not lost for us, either.

Several times during that day Emma went out into the streets then came back with news. "They say the British navy is sailing up the bay. They will attack by water." Then another time: "The men at the docks say Ross's army has been seen landing at North Point."

"Ah!" the doctor cried gleefully. "The British will take the city by sea and by land at the same time. We will crush Baltimore like a piece of rotting fruit under our heels!"

I looked worriedly at Mama.

"Courage, my girl," she whispered again. "Courage."

That night, the bombardment began. We heard the British ships firing on Baltimore, and the huge guns of Fort McHenry booming back in answer. From our prison on Boston Street, there was no way for us to tell how badly the city was being hit. But through the window, which Macaphee had at last reopened to allow in fresh air, we could see the blinding flares of the bombs in the night sky.

Our captor grew more and more restless as the hours passed. He paced the floor, checking and rechecking the pistol and ammunition he'd taken from Sean. I knew he was anxious to go out into the city and see for himself what was happening, but he was nervous about leaving us.

At last he said to his sister, "I must discover how the attack proceeds. I expected the Americans to surrender after an hour or less, but this maddening barrage goes on and on."

"What about *them*?" she demanded, narrowing her eyes at Mama and me. "There's two of 'em.

What's to stop 'em from overpowering me?"

"This," he said, handing her the pistol. "You just sit yourself in front of that door. If either of them gives you the least trouble, you shoot the girl." He leveled a cold glare my way, and I shivered for I knew he meant what he said.

"Not the mother?" Emma asked, looking disappointed.

"No!" he shouted, whirling around to face her. His face was as red as his hair. "*The girl,* you lamebrained ninny! The girl! Margaret won't do anything if she thinks her daughter might be hurt. Now just do as I say and I'll be back within the hour."

Emma cautiously took the pistol from him and, as soon as he'd left, dragged one of the chairs in front of the door. She sat down in it and glared sourly at the straw mat where Mama and I sat.

Now, I thought, is our best chance. Perhaps our only chance.

I glanced at Mama and could see she understood. But fear filled her soft eyes, and she shook her head at me. "Caroline—" she warned.

I ignored her and stood up. I'd been thinking for the past hour that the key to our freedom was discovering a way to make Emma discharge her weapon at some worthless object instead of at one of us. Then the pistol would be useless, for it could be shot only once. I doubted she knew how to reload it, even if her brother had left ammunition.

I strolled across the room toward the window. Emma's eyes narrowed suspiciously.

I had started to turn back toward the mat, still plotting my next move, when the door behind Emma flew open with tremendous force. The rough wooden panel knocked both the woman and her chair into the middle of the room with a deafening crash. The pistol jumped from her fingers and rattled across the floor before skidding to a stop beneath the table.

Into the room rushed a monstrous figure in tattered clothing. "Jake!" I cried happily. Behind him came Charlie.

Jake grabbed Emma before she could pick herself up off the floor. I crawled under the table and seized the pistol. "I've got it!" I shouted. Turning around, I saw Mama staring in amazement at Charlie.

She smiled softly and whispered, "It's true . . . it's true." Tears of joy trickled down her cheeks.

Charlie limped over to her, and they hugged tightly, Mama crying on Charlie's shoulder for as long as Jake would leave them to their reunion.

"Come along, come along now . . . plenty of time for that!" he scolded. "We best be off before that Judas brother of hers comes back."

"Wait!" Emma cried. "Lawrence will kill me if he finds I've let them go!"

"He might," I agreed, remembering what he'd done to Sean.

Charlie bit down on his lip and nodded at Jake.

The waterman pulled a black cloak off a hook on the wall and handed it to Emma. "Then, girl, you best be gettin' yourself far away from Bawl'imer and your brother, fast as you can."

He shoved her out the door, into the street, just as I was remembering where I'd seen her before—in the woods near Elk Ridge. The woman in brown. She'd been watching us for her brother while he was away on his espionage missions. She'd also probably brought him news of troops and supplies from Baltimore to pass along to the British.

We left on foot, for the carriage was gone, Macaphee having taken it to search for news of the battle. Charlie still couldn't run very well on his injured leg. But we moved on foot as quickly as possible through the city streets, working our way around the harbor's edge, dodging wagons, militias, and small herds of sheep and goats. The animals had been brought into the city to supply food for its defenders, in case of a lengthy siege.

The night air was thick with blue-gray powder blown in from the discharges of the cannons. I found it difficult to breathe without choking; my eyes burned and felt gritty.

Across the water I could barely make out the fort, silhouetted against the hazy night by the light of every exploding shell. Most of the missiles seemed to fall short of the battlements, plummeting harmlessly into the water. But the noise of their bursting was no less terrifying.

"How did you find us?" I cried at Charlie as we rushed over slippery cobbles.

"Mr. Black!" Charlie shouted back. Jake lumbered along beside him, his big arm around Mama to keep her from stumbling. "He sent two boys on horseback to follow your carriage and find out where you'd been taken. Black came not far behind, met with his boys, then found Jake and me. He told us where you'd be."

But I was still confused. "How did Mr. Black know you were alive? How did he know where to find you? I didn't tell him or anyone else at Elk Ridge."

"Sean," Charlie said, a mysterious glimmer in his eyes. "Sean Foley told him."

I stopped dead in the street while the others rushed on. After a dizzying moment, I ran to catch up with Charlie and tugged at his sleeve. "That's . . . that's impossible!" I cried. "Sean wouldn't have given up your secret before Macaphee took us. And by then he had been shot dead!"

Charlie winked at me. "He was shot, but not quite dead, sister. Cook and Mr. Black took care of him. The bullet struck the boy's arm. He'll live, they say."

I stopped running because I felt like putting all my energy into a grin, and there wasn't enough strength left in me to do both at once.

Jake reached out and dragged me along. "Don't stop movin', girl-y-oh!" he shouted above an earth-quaking boom. "We best find shelter and wait out this battle."

Charlie brought us to a stable a few blocks back of the docks. It appeared to have been abandoned by its owner; no livestock remained. Twenty or so men with their arms were making use of the empty stalls to catch a few hours' sleep before the fierce hand-to-hand battle everyone foresaw for the morning. We found an unoccupied corner, and I helped Charlie put down fresh straw. When we'd finished, Charlie sat between Mama and me, one arm around each of us.

I felt truly happy for the first time in many months. I thought, We are a family again . . . if only for these few hours. For, by dawn, who could say if any of us would be alive.

☆ BY DAWN'S EARLY LIGHT ☆

IT WAS THE SILENCE THAT WOKE ME. FOR A MOMENT I tried to remember where I was and what had caused the terrifying explosions in my dreams. Then I recalled the deafening cannonade from Fort McHenry, the enemy's bombs blazing against the night sky . . . our proud, immense flag that taunted the British, as if daring them to attack.

Mama still slept in the straw. Jake had gone off somewhere, and so had the men from the militia. But Charlie leaned against the worm-riddled planks of the stable door, looking out into the morning mists off the harbor. The air still smelled metallic from the powder, but the dense charcoal haze had started to thin.

"What has happened?" I asked. "Is the battle over? Have we surrendered?"

"Come see," Charlie said, beckoning to me.

I went over and stood beside him. He rested an arm over my shoulders. Together we looked out over the city's rooftops from the stable on the hill. From here, in the daylight, most of the harbor and all of the fort on the other side could be seen. The enormous red, white, and blue banner still waved over the stone walls and the wooden barracks they surrounded. The British ships had retreated into a wider part of the bay, their prows pointing toward the sea.

"They're leaving?" I cried in disbelief.

"We shall see," Charlie said. I heard in his voice very little of the boy I'd grown up with. He sounded all man. He sounded like our father—serious, calm, and thoughtful.

"Oh, Charlie, if they go away, perhaps they will never come back. And we will have no more wars."

He blinked and sighed. "There is still Ross's army

on North Point. A messenger arrived while you slept, summoning the men to muster around the other side of the harbor to meet the British infantry."

"How long ago was that?" I asked.

"Hours," he said quietly. "Now all we can do is wait. In the meantime, we should look for something to eat."

"I don't want to wake Mama," I said. "She has had an awful shock—believing you dead, now seeing you alive."

Charlie gave me a crooked smile. "There was no other way to protect the two of you but to pretend Captain Moses's plot to kill me had worked. I didn't know who was behind it until Mr. Black told me that Sean had been shot, and you and Mama taken away by Macaphee."

I shivered, then frowned as more questions assaulted me. "Why did they wait so long to try to kill you? You were aboard the *Liberty* for weeks."

Charlie shrugged. "Probably to make it look more like an accident. If they disposed of me right away, it might have aroused suspicion. Captain Moses must have been worried about being discovered as a spy. Apparently, he was already under suspicion by some in the navy. He had been a trader when that paid best. Then a privateer when he could make more money sinking British ships. The British must have offered him a generous bribe to ferry information from Macaphee to them."

"So he gave up his country for money but he wasn't willing to give his life for either side."

"Right," Charlie said. "He and Macaphee are cut of the same cloth."

"It's odd that no one ever questioned the doctor," I murmured. "We all thought his trips quite normal since everyone was busy trying to protect his family and property from the British."

"He was clever in that way," Charlie agreed.

"But not so much in others. His pride and greed were his ruin."

"Yes."

I thought for a moment. "He seemed almost as desperate to keep Mama's trust as he was to keep the government's. If his choice of a ship and captain for you looked like a good one at first, she would be grateful and maybe marry him."

"Then," Charlie added, "he'd have Elk Ridge and the Dorsey fortune."

"He kept trying to make her give him a writ, to allow him to draw all of Papa's and Grandpapa's money from the banks," I remembered. "That was after he'd asked her to marry him, and she'd turned him down. One way or another, he was determined to make himself a rich man."

Charlie chuckled. "I guess he hadn't counted on my little sister standing in his way."

My cheeks grew warm with pride. "I just didn't believe you were dead, that's all."

From the straw came a groan. Mama sat up and frowned at us. Slowly, the perplexed glaze slid away from her eyes, and she smiled at Charlie. "It's true," she whispered. "Thank God it wasn't just a dream."

"Are you hungry?" Charlie asked.

"*I* am starving!" I cried before Mama could answer.

"I suppose we could all use some food," she agreed, standing up to brush the straw out of her skirts. "But if what Emma said is true, we won't find much."

"We have friends," Charlie said. "Come along."

I took Mama's hand and followed Charlie out of the stable. "What about Jake?"

"He'll meet us where we're headed," he said.

As we descended the narrow streets to the harbor's edge, growing crowds milled about on corners. People were talking in excited voices, waving weapons or their hands, pointing at the sky where the British bombs had burst during the night, or at the finger of land to the southeast, where Ross's army was said to be marching toward Baltimore. They all looked ready to do battle as soon as the enemy showed their faces.

A man broke into the midst of a large group of people. He was shouting, but the words were so garbled that I couldn't understand them. He gestured wildly toward a nearby alley.

Turning, I peered between the brick walls and saw a most horrid sight. A mob of people had crushed into the narrow space and were throwing stones and broken bricks at a lump on the ground, cursing the thing that twisted and flailed helplessly as the missiles battered it.

I started toward them, but Charlie grabbed my shoulder and held me back. "Don't. You can't stop a crowd gone mad like that. You'll be hurt, Carrie."

"Oh, dear," Mama breathed as a man's boot jerked out from beneath the pile of clothing and arms flew up to protect a bloodied face. "What could the poor creature have done to deserve such treatment? They're killing him!"

"He's a turncoat, missus," a farmer standing on the curb said. "He was caught carrying a letter to General Ross."

Between shifting legs of attackers I glimpsed a familiar shock of red hair. I staggered backward, sickened by the sight, but strangely satisfied, too—for Macaphee was being punished not unjustly for his treachery and greed.

Whether or not Charlie or Mama realized who the traitor was, I couldn't be sure. I chose not to ask.

"Have you heard news of Ross's march on the city?"

Charlie asked the farmer, his voice tight with worry.

Surprisingly, the stranger grinned at him. "Boy, don't you know?"

"Know what?" I asked.

"Ross has been shot off his horse by two farm boys yonder on North Point. Poor lads were killed right away by British soldiers, but Ross lies dying, if he isn't already gone. His troops are in retreat."

Charlie turned to me, a look of amazement in his eyes.

I could barely believe it myself. "Does this mean we've won?" I shouted.

Charlie hugged me. "If we haven't won the war, we've at least survived the battle. The coming days will tell the rest."

Charlie was right, and so was our president. Winning a war isn't as simple as beating a friend at a chess game. Although the British gave up trying to take Baltimore after losing their commanding general and failing to bomb Fort McHenry into submission, they sent smaller raiding parties to attack a few towns along the bay. In every instance, the citizens fought them off.

President and Mrs. Madison found refuge in Virginia after their home had been burned. Mr. Madison sent Mr. John Quincy Adams and our friends, Henry Clay and Albert Gallatin, along with two other men, to Ghent in Belgium. There they met with British commissioners to try to agree on a treaty that would bring peace between America and England.

Meanwhile, the fighting continued, although it was not near Baltimore and some of it actually happened after the war was officially over. We learned that our General Andrew Jackson fought the British at New Orleans the following January and won a stunning victory. Word of the American triumph arrived in Washington well before news that the Treaty of Ghent had been signed in December. If only ships could cross the ocean in less than two months, Jackson's men wouldn't have had to fight at all.

Some said the War of 1812 was a war nobody won, for neither side gained or lost land, and both governments remained the same as before the war.

The English didn't even promise to leave our ships and sailors alone. But I thought a lot had changed, even though it didn't show up on papers signed by important men. We Americans had proven ourselves. We had shown the British we were a country that would stand up for its citizens' rights. We had won the world's respect.

I left for Philadelphia in February, after enjoying a much longer vacation from school than any of the other students, who had only the usual month of September. During my remaining time at Elk Ridge, I helped Mama return furniture and our other belongings to their proper places in the main house. Paintings had to be rehung, mirrors uncovered and cleaned, silver and porcelain unpacked.

Charlie and I went riding nearly every day, and his leg began to mend more quickly with rest, exercise, and good nourishment. He talked wistfully of returning to the sea, and I sensed he would be gone as soon as he was well and had found a solid ship with room for him in the crew.

Sean sometimes accompanied us on horseback, for he enjoyed a special status in the household since his brave attempt to rescue Mama and me from Macaphee. His duties were made lighter, and Mr. Black treated him with respect I'd never seen him give any man or boy in his charge. Although Sean's arm eventually healed, he said it sometimes ached with changing weather.

Amelia was waiting in our shared room upstairs when Sean delivered me to Mrs. Brown's boarding-house in Philadelphia. "*Mon Dieu*, he is twice as handsome as you described in your letters," she gasped, staring out the second-floor window at Sean as he unloaded the carriage.

I shrugged, pretending indifference. "Perhaps."

"It is a pity he is a servant. I sense you are very fond of him from your letters, *ma chérie*."

"He would have died for Mama and me. We owe him a great deal." As if that were all there was to it.

"Ah," she responded, but I could tell by the twinkle in her blue eyes she wasn't fooled. "Still, it is a shame he is not a freeman, with property. He would make such a pretty suitor with that black-black hair and eyes so dark and quiet."

"I expect he will be released from his indenture very soon," I commented lightly.

"How so? Your letter, it said he owes your grandfather four more years."

"He does, but I wrote Grandpapa in Belgium." I avoided her eyes but felt them boring into me, demanding an explanation. I sighed. "Mama said that my grandfather probably wouldn't release Sean early, even though he'd nearly been killed trying to rescue us. Grandpapa believes it's every servant's duty to defend his master's family. So I gave him another reason to end Sean's indenture."

"What did you *do*, Caroline?" Amelia asked, her voice thick with suspicion, trembling with curiosity. "Did you plead with him?"

"No."

"Did you invent grand tales to win the courageous fellow's freedom?"

I shook my head and smiled at my folded hands

on the windowsill. "No. I just told the truth."

"The truth?"

"Yes," I said casually. "Sean Foley has a terrible temper. He is willful and stubborn, and he argues every instruction. I advised my grandfather that he'd do well to get rid of the obnoxious fellow as soon as possible, as Sean would continue to make life miserable for all of us at Elk Ridge. And no sane landholder would pay even a dollar for his contract."

Amelia shook a finger at me. "But that's a lie, Caroline."

"No, it's not." I looked fondly down at the Irish boy as he lifted hat boxes, a jewelry case, and bag of needlework from the carriage. Even from inside the house I could hear him cursing the uselessness of female decorations as the containers tumbled from his arms into the gutter. A warm glow filled [illegible]s and I smiled so hard my cheeks hurt. "Sean Foley, you see, is a very poor servant. But he will make a very fine freeman."